TALES
OF THE
MASTER
RACE

MARCIE HERSHMAN

HarperPerennial
A Division of HarperCollinsPublishers

"Warning!"; "Distribution of Clocks"; "Protective Custody Order: J. Flintrop" from *Concentration Camp Dachau: 1933–1945,* © 1979 by Comité International de Dachau. (Dachau Memorial Archives)

"Questionaire 1," from *The Nazi Doctors: Medical Killing and the Psychology of Genocide,* © 1986 by Robert J. Lifton. Reprinted by permission of Basic Books, a division of HarperCollins Publishers.

"A Lively Youngster" and excerpt from "The Honor Cross of the German Mother," from *Nazi Culture,* © 1966 by George Mosse, Schocken Books, 1981. Reprinted by permission of George Mosse.

Excerpt from the diary of Louise Solmitz, from *Documents on Nazism, 1919-1945,* © 1974 by Jeremy Noakes and Geoffry Pridham, Viking Press, 1975.

Letter from Alfried Krupp von Bohlen, from *Less Than Slaves,* © 1979 by Benjamin B. Ferencz, Harvard University Press.

The author wishes to thank the Brookline Public Library, Brookline, Massachusetts, a wonderful resource.

Portions of this book have appeared in *Tikkun* and *American Fiction.*

A hardcover edition of this book was published in 1991 by HarperCollins Publishers.

First HarperPerennial edition published 1992.

Designed by C. Linda Dingler

The Library of Congress has catalogued the hardcover edition as follows:

Hershman, Marcie, 1951–
    Tales of the master race / by Marcie Hershman.—1st ed.
    p. cm.
    ISBN 0-06-016644-4
    1. Germany—History—1933–1945—Fiction. I. Title.
  PS3558.E777T3 1991
  813'.54—dc20   90-56363

ISBN 0-06-092353-9 (pbk.)
92 93 94 95 96 CC/RRD 10 9 8 7 6 5 4 3

TALES OF THE MASTER RACE

In memory of Anna Pollak Weiss

whose stories, love, and spirit
spoke to her granddaughter

Acknowledgments

I'm grateful to these friends: My brother, Robert Hersh-man, who one day, out of the blue, asked me to travel to Munich with him. Eileen Pollack and Dan Wakefield, who read each one of my drafts and kept my courage up. Ellen Levine, who stuck by me for years and guided this book on its way. Ted Solotaroff, who gave me the thoughtful support every writer needs. And Rebecca Blunk, whose presence throughout this long process has made all the difference.

TALES OF THE MASTER RACE

Sworn Statement
79-4328

Why did you decide to live in Kreiswald?

What made you continue to stay?

When you say it was "home," what does that mean to you?

You mention friends and job—anything else?

Define "comfortable" for me.

So, if it was comfortable in the way life was lived—the habits and customs you mention and so on, how did that change during—let's say especially during—1939 to 1945?

Can we talk about it in general, if you can't recall too much that's specific? How would that be for you?

Then, what else would you want to talk about?

What else would you want to talk about?

Can you recall—can you recall anything else about that time except that so many things, in general, were difficult for everyone?

What does that—"suffered"—mean?

You say people were hungry. What else?

What else were they? I mean, for example—what did you—what did you see on the streets?

The streets of Kreiswald, what did you see happening on them that you can recall, that seems to stick with you, even today?

Sadness?

What does that—"sadness"—mean?

So, people—people—so, people didn't look happy. Do people look happy on the streets today?

I see. They're better off—prosperous. And back then they weren't. But what else were people, then?

I mean, during those years we're talking about. Don't rush. I have time, I can wait.

Why weren't they curious?

You don't want to get specific? What don't you want to be specific about?

What don't you want to be specific about?

What don't you want to be specific about?

What secrets? Tell me about them.

All right, so you knew there were secrets, but you didn't know specifically what they were, is that it?

Do you know these secrets, now?

How did you find out about them?

Newspapers, current newspapers—and how else?

Newspapers and the new politicians' speeches and—?

And files?

What files are those?

The files belonging to all the authorities? What was in them?

You think there were the usual things. You think official documents, just information and—and personal statements, sworn statements.

Tell me about them, if you can.

What do you mean by the term "rubbish"?

Lies? What does that—"lies"—mean?

So, anyone can tamper with documents? Anyone can make up some few facts, some history, some statements?

But if the statements were sworn to, if people swore that they were true, then—?

No, they were lies? Just pieces of paper, just ink? Just lies?

You believe everything found was made up of lies? Hundreds and thousands of lies, all piled atop each other. All of them. You believe none of what was found in those files, why should you?

Does that mean that the secrets you knew about, then, those were lies, too?

Were the secrets you knew back then lies?

Sorry, it's confusing. I remember now that you said you only learned about the secrets from the newspapers, afterward. The newspapers informed you about the files, about the statements in the files. All right.

Well, tell me what other people thought. Yes, about the files exposed in the newspapers.

Well, did they—did people get together and talk about them?

What about in their homes, what about there?

Why didn't people want to talk about them? What excuse did they give?

What does that mean: the winners wrote the articles?

So, winners can say whatever they want about the losers? With power, you can make up anything, erase anything you want? You say: it is always like that.

Did you believe what the people in power told you then?

Back then, yes—did you believe—

You didn't.

What did you think was a lie, back then?

The Jews and all weren't really to blame for all of your country's trouble. You believe that was a lie, that they were to blame.

What do you think happened to the people who didn't have power?

What happened to those people who were lied about?

They were taken away? Where were they taken?

You don't know—how could you know? You stayed right here.

All you knew is they had gone.

Did anything else happen to people, any of the ones who were lied about, besides being taken away?

Tell me what was found in some basements.

Decapitated bodies?

They were in prison uniforms?

Was this reported in the newspapers now or back then?

You aren't sure. You must have read it afterward.

Warnung!

Am 30. Mai wurden an der Umgebungsmauer des Konzentrationslagers in Dachau zwei Personen beobachtet, die versuchten, über die Mauer hinwegzuschauen. Selbstverständlich wurden sie sofort festgenommen. Sie erklärten, aus Neugierde, wie das Lager von innen aussehe, über die Mauer geschaut zu haben. Um ihren Wissensdurst befriedigen zu können, und ihnen hiezu Gelegenheit zu geben, wurden sie eine Nacht im Konzentrationslager behalten.

Hoffentlich ist ihre Neugierde nunmehr befriedigt, wenn dies auch auf etwas unvorhergesehene Weise geschehen ist.

Sollten weitere Neugierige sich nicht abhalten lassen, dem Verbot zuwiderhandelnd über die Mauer zu schauen, so sei ihnen jetzt schon zur Befriedigung ihrer Neugierde mitgeteilt, daß die Folgenden nicht nur eine Nacht, sondern länger Gelegenheit zum Studium des Lagers bekommen werden.

Neugierige sind hiemit nochmals gewarnt.

Der Beauftragte der obersten SA-Führung:
Sonderkommissar Friederichs.

Warning!

On May 30, two persons were observed trying to look over the wall surrounding the concentration camp in Dachau. They were of course immediately arrested. They explained that they had been curious to see what the camp looked like inside. In order to give them the opportunity to satisfy their curiosity they were detained overnight. It is hoped that their curiosity has now been satisfied in spite of this unforeseen measure. We wish to still the curiosity of all those who might ignore this warning by informing them that in the future they will be given the opportunity of studying the camp from inside for longer than just one night.
All inquisitive persons are hereby warned once more.

In charge of the Supreme S.A. Command
Special Commissioner Friedrichs
Amper Bote. No 129, June 2, 1933

The Guillotine

YOU'D THINK we've been told everything about those twelve years, but that isn't so. History, like any lover, is selective in the facts it reveals about its beloved. And so, though the French Revolution's guillotine is always noted, the Third Reich's is not. The Third Reich, of course, had other methods of execution; but, as I say, it also had guillotines. Eleven of them. Hardworking, swift, sharp, silent. The blades sliced through the necks not of innocent Jews or gypsies or homosexuals but of those who were then called Aryans. Germans. Only Germans. In eleven different locations around the country, often in the basement of a district police station, men and women were put to death, one by one by one. Probably the guillotine brought no more solitary a death than did any other method; still it was horrible, and even without a whisper campaign, lots of people knew that lives were being cut off in those basements, in that way. We didn't need to talk about it; we only needed to know it.

The authorities, such as they were, understood that.

"A little knowledge," Commander Terskan used to say, "is

just enough." He was a swarthy, two-chinned, but not unat-
tractive man. He'd sit at the main desk and bring the blades
of his scissors together. The sound of those blue-tinged shears
crossing each other raised the small hairs on the back of my
neck, just as it did when I sat at the barber's.

Rolf Terskan understood that. It was his little joke in those
first months when he knew that someone was scheduled
below. "Torgood, you need a trim. Even Gruber's night
clerk doesn't look this lax. How did your wife let you out of
the house like this? Doesn't she inspect you?"

"I stand a good head taller than she does, Commander
Terskan. She can't get the necessary perspective."

"Yes, well, I'm the only inspector who matters, anyway,"
he'd say, as if I'd actually replied to his admonishment with
anything approaching the truth. After all, Gerda did not see
me only when we were standing. "Come here, day clerk
Stella. Bend down."

Gently, his splay-fingered right hand would push my head
forward. Then the shears' cool metal would seem to exhale—
again that shiver down in my collar—and the hairs would fall
like insects in a pile of faint brown lines on the floor. Invari-
ably, from below, one minute later or five, by which time I
was already sweeping up, there would be a thump. Sometimes, preceding it, there would also be a shout: *No!* or *I
won't!* But the cry was always quickly cut off. I hated to be
on my knees when anything happened below. I could always
feel it right through my bones. To take in some poor soul's
death through your kneecaps makes you want to beg mercy
for yourself, because you know when you stand, it's in you.
A small tremor you can't shake.

This was at a time when the newspaper was filled daily
with stories of violence. Many of the incidents took place in
the center of Kreiswald—and many of them on Bergenstrasse. As the *Kompass* reported one incident: "The shop-

owners Edelmann and Rosenbaum were ordered to wait. Both of the so-called chosen foolishly disobeyed the order and tried to run." Even the letters in these words looked ugly—thin and slanted, pressed into formation. You think because we lived in the middle of those twelve years that we didn't see hate anymore? Not so. We saw it but we pretended, with that little whisper of knowledge—the same rasp that told us about the guillotine at work under the police station floor—that such slight awareness was good. The hairbreadth was what kept us safe. No more and no less. Any more awareness and we might be compelled into taking a dangerous stance; any less and we'd be screaming, *Filth out! One people! One country!*—the same phrases that blackened the pages of what once was simply a town newspaper.

Commander Terskan would brush the stray hairs off my shoulders. "Raise your head," he'd say. "Let me see my work." Then after a slight pause would come: "Yes, you're as good as new. When you go home tonight, see if your wife isn't thankful that I kept my hand steady."

But my face, those evenings, was no welcome sight.

"No." And, biting her lip, Gerda would turn away—to a table or stove or vase, seeking some task in which to bury her gaze.

I'd enter the door left open behind her. Because I still wanted the embrace we usually shared, I'd follow her back into the house. "It happened again, Gerda." I'd speak quickly. "Two of them. A man and a woman."

She paused at the hall table. Her hand went for the geraniums in the clay pot. "Commander Terskan told you that?"

"He didn't. But it was quiet and I heard."

"So you didn't see them." She examined the underside of the leaves for mites.

"Of course not. They were downstairs. I told you, that's where it happens."

"And you have no part in any of it?"

I came and stood next to her. "Gerda, I'm the file clerk. Surely you realize what little that means."

She plucked a dead bloom off one of the plants. She looked like she was going to cry.

"Rolf Terskan kept me busy upstairs. You can see that well enough! Here's the proof." I leaned in toward her.

"I saw. You have one of those haircuts again. It's a terrible job, too short at your ears."

"But it proves that I was upstairs the entire time. That nothing else happened to me. If you think of it that way, it's not terrible, is it? I'm sure that's why he does it. That has to be the reason."

"But—" her voice wavered. "Your ears, they're, oh, I don't know! It frightens me to see you like this."

She looked up. Her face was so sweet, a nineteen-year-old who so earnestly wanted to believe in our innocence, in what was so obviously the case, and *yet*—yet she was not the nineteen she could have been. But I wasn't the twenty-six I could have been, either.

"Better to see me like this than not at all." I moved to put my arms around her.

"Go and wash," she said, her voice harsh. "The cuttings are still on you. They get in our bed, too. I hate it, how they can be that tiny and still jab and prick."

"No one likes it," I replied. "What do you think? And I was going to clean up, you don't need to prod me."

In our bedroom, I stripped to the waist. The whiteness of the porcelain washbowl seemed a relief. When the water was dripping off my nose and chin, I opened my eyes: her face was in front of me, caught in the small shaving mirror tacked to the wall.

"Gerda?" A little water trickled into my mouth.

"I'm sorry," she said from behind me. "I'm glad for how well you look."

I didn't move, just stayed bent over like that.

She stepped closer. Her lips brushed my bare shoulder as if it were a relic. "Sometimes talking is a mistake. You mustn't take my words to heart, especially since I said everything wrong. It really is a good job."

She put her fingers through my hair and shook out the clear drops. "Rolf Terskan is such a complex man, isn't he? I don't know what to make of him." She rubbed the bar of soap, working the lather into my scalp. "I used an extra ration coupon for our meal, so there's some pork in the stew. If I pour some of it into the blue pot will you take it to him tomorrow? About what he's been doing for you, Torgood, will you thank him for me?"

Her fingers in my hair were loving, entangled. She had delicate hands, fine bones, as if she were a watchmaker's daughter, or a musician's. But her father had worked in an iron foundry. In 1934, when she was fifteen, a finished rod slid off a cart and hit him square in the chest. Gerda was the second of six children. She and Christoph, the eldest boy, were taken from school. Christoph went into the foundry and Gerda to a clothing factory. Her hands were used to guide fabrics under the needles of the huge, electric-driven machines. When we were courting, she'd tell me how it was to work there. Sometimes, she'd say, fights would break out. In the monotony and din, a girl would seize another girl's hand and try to push it under the needles as if it were a piece of fabric. The fight rarely took long and it never ended in blood. In fact, the girls were usually giddy with relief as they returned to their stations. The work that only moments before had provoked them became simple and clear—even, it could be said, joyful. The brown Nazi cloth flew beneath the workers' fingers.

I didn't like thinking of Gerda there. Much better to see her, at seventeen, bending over the flats of nubby orange begonias and rangy spices in the plant nursery. She got that job just a week after we married. Neither of us could believe our luck, how saying *Yes* aloud changed our lives. Everything was new and moist. Everything smelled sweet, with a kind of deep thickness, like the soil in those square nursery flats, which never dries out and looks as dark and luscious as a seven-layer cake.

"Torgood, always," she'd whisper in my ear those first nights. "Oh, beloved." Enfolding her, my whole body would sting with the pleasure. So many nights are part of the first nights, it seems impossible to pry them apart, each from each. Of course, history can do that. History can separate the first from the second night, the first from the second fact. Memory, softhearted and perhaps not as shrewd as its more public relative, just wants to hold things intact.

With a shiver, I reached up from the washbowl and touched Gerda's wrist, damp from the drops of soapy water.

Her skin slid across my fingers. "The towels," she said. "I don't want you to get chilled."

She wrapped the short one, turbanlike, about my head. The second, bulkier, went over my shoulders. "Stand up and you're done."

I turned around, damp-eyed, blinking. "All right?"

She gave the makeshift headdress an affectionate pat. "Much better. Very good."

"Maybe I'll keep wearing them. I can see you like me wrapped up this way."

Smiling, she tucked the second towel up under my chin. "That would be very silly."

Yet I did stay cosseted. While our kitchen stove sent out waves of heat, a sultan waved his right arm, and his wife, laughing, obeyed his every whim.

"How very kind," said Rolf Terskan, when he saw the blue pot on his desk the next morning. Using thumb and forefinger, he plucked a pink-flecked bone halfway out. "I hope you have enough for yourselves or I couldn't accept such a gift."

"We're fine, Commander Terskan. There's only the two of us. Gerda very much wants you to have this."

He smiled and let the bone sink back under the curls of carrots and cabbage. "Her handiwork in response to my own? Please give her my warm regards. I wasn't expecting anything in return."

"I will."

He rubbed the dot of yellowish gravy between his thumb and forefinger as if it were a lotion, and shifted in the chair to take a handkerchief from his back pocket. "How is she, by the way? Well?"

"Why, yes. Why?"

"When she was here last Friday, she looked a little pale around the edges. As if she expected someone to leap out and grab her. She actually trembled." Marveling, Commander Terskan shook out the handkerchief. "I made her sit down in my chair and we talked. You were out, taking some letters to post. Obviously, she didn't mention it to you."

"She might have," I said, a little surprised.

"Well, I'm glad she forgot about it. Some people seem to find it hard, being in the station; I understand that. Unfortunately, the police can't protect everyone." He sat back in his chair with a thin smile. "Gerda's very sweet, but delicate. Does she know what goes on underneath here?"

"Most people seem to have their suspicions, Commander Terskan."

"They do," he said, "don't they? Which is why I wouldn't allow the outside world into the house. Work should be work, not part of the home, that's my understanding of it. When I take a wife, which I will, I'll make sure the two stay separate. She won't see anything that might shake her confidence, her sense of security." He paused. "Do you tell her anything?"

I took a breath and said, "I would never breach any security matters. But some days, because of how I look when I come home—the haircuts, I suppose—I have to say at least something. She can see the change, you know."

"You tell her." He shook his large head. "I thought so, I thought you might do that. You shouldn't, Torgood. It's weak."

"It's hard to keep things from your wife."

"Is it?" he mused.

"Besides," I said, "she wants to know."

"Well, I didn't find that to be the case. When she was here, two prisoners, a man and a woman, were being brought to the basement. I heard the bulkhead door creaking. Gerda had just started to listen—you know how that is, don't you—so I took charge and distracted her. We talked about inconsequential things. Of course, when she left, it was with a much lighter heart than when she'd entered. It made me feel very good about myself, to relieve her of unnecessary concerns." He eyed me.

My scalp prickled as if the shears had come too close. "Thank you, Commander Terskan."

He paused and flicked his pencil at the cast-iron lid of the pot. He set up a kind of rhythm, then said, "There's some nasty business in front of you now. A change in orders. It came early this morning with the new prisoner." He withdrew an envelope from his middle drawer. "Read it at your desk."

I took one look at the top sheet and thrust my chair back. "Commander Terskan!" I leaned, palms down, on the blotter.

"I wish I could countermand them. But at this level, I can't."

"But this." I jabbed at the paper. "Who would give this to me? I take down people's words."

Commander Terskan blew the air out of his lips, but even as he exhaled, his cheeks puffed out, saving some air, as a squirrel saves seeds, for a time when the supply might be scarce. "And from now on, you'll take down bodily details, too. Your duties have expanded from the mere taking of statements. You'll record head measurements, weights, partial and otherwise. You'll see, it's all written there."

Actually, I never even took direct statements. How could I, when I never saw the prisoners? Prudmann, on the night shift, probably never saw the inmates either. Simply, the job involved stamping the papers forwarded to us: *Received on such-and-such a date, at such-and-such an hour; Kreiswald Police; Kreiswald, Germany.* The statements, such as they were, had been given first to the police at the arresting station, and again perhaps to a clerk at the trial. By the time the prisoners arrived here, there was no more to say. All of us understood it: not only had their history preceded them, it had already absorbed them.

Commander Terskan walked over to the file cabinet against the back wall. "Come here, I'll show you something—that is, if Gruber's assistant hasn't mislaid it. Sharing information usually leads to some kind of mistake."

From the top drawer, he pulled out the first report. He showed it to me on the flat of his palm. "And this is just one case." Flipping open the cardboard folder, he rifled among the sheets until he found what he wanted. " 'Wendist, Herman H.,' " he read in a neutral tone. " 'Twenty-six. Aryan.

Catholic. Social Democrat. Educated at Hamburg University in biology.' Do you know why he was beheaded? It was in January."

"I don't remember the statement."

"He was a traitor. He was overheard urging his fellow workers in a munitions factory to engage in sabotage. He said he could show them how to assemble weapons so they would misfire. You don't know the half of it, what that means. A neighbor's boy, say, or maybe it's your cousin, he takes aim with that gun, in Czechoslovakia or in Poland, and what happens? That should concern you, even with your medical exemption."

My mouth was dry. "I have a bad lung."

"I know." He put the file back and closed the drawer. "But should we keep a traitor housed and fed at the expense of helping our good people?" He gave me a measured look. "I know how generous Gerda was to fill up that pot for me. She gave, from her own shelves, a real gift. I won't squander it."

He put his hand on my shoulder. "Listen to me. What happens to most people is their own doing. People commit unspeakable acts and someone, who they don't even know is watching, sees them doing it and saves them from doing it again by punishing them for it. The punishments vary according to the crime, but it all works out in the end." He gave me a gentle squeeze. "You'll see I'm right. It won't be as difficult to bear as you think."

"When?" I asked.

"Soon. Tomorrow, eight in the morning. Do you want to read his file?" Commander Terskan went over to his desk and picked up the stew pot; the folder lay beneath it. "There's only a confession in it. You'll add the other details." He hesitated a moment before dropping it into my hands.

I brought it to my desk. The pot had pressed its shape into the greyish cover. I couldn't bring myself to turn past it, as if by tilting that imprinted circle, cabbage and watery meat would actually spill out, leaving my fingers slick, my pants and shoes spattered. So I didn't open it.

The morning went on. The station filled and emptied with people and their complaints. A vagrant was brought in and held for questioning since he could be a Jew trying to get through town without the proper permits. A grocer named a neighborhood boy for stealing an apple. Two fistfights were reported. A dead mare was reported lying off Grubenplatz, and both its owner and identifying livery were gone. Citizens said that they wanted the beast carted from their street as soon as possible.

It was noon when I looked up from the typewriter to see Gerda enter. She was wearing her good thick wool sweater and brown skirt and she held her shoulders back in a way that meant she was unsure but didn't want to appear to be. In her left hand were gloves and shopping bag. She came halfway in, then stopped.

"A pleasure," said Commander Terskan, scraping his chair back. He walked around to the front of his desk and greeted her with a short bow. "Now I can thank you in person."

She flushed and gave him a hesitant smile. "You're welcome, Commander Terskan. I hope you'll enjoy it, though it's little enough. I mean, compared with all that you do for us."

"I never expected it," he said. "So to me it is generous indeed. It looks delicious."

She colored even more.

"I plan to have it for my dinner tonight."

"Oh, please don't rush. Keep the pot until you're done."

"I'll do no such thing." He reprimanded her lightly. "I have too many pots at my house, more than one person can use. There's no need for you to go without. Tomorrow you shall have it back, personally washed."

"But I can't imagine you washing a pot!"

"Can't you?" He tilted his head. "Well, now you will have to, won't you?" And he held up his palms.

She glanced away from them, laughing in a kind of pained delight.

"Gerda, what is it?" I called from my desk. "Come here."

She faltered. "Commander Terskan—?"

"Go, of course." With a smile, he waved her on.

"What do you want?" I kept my voice low.

She withdrew a roll and lunchmeat from the bag. "You took the gift for the commander but forgot your own meal." She laid the sandwich directly on top of the folder I'd been trying to avoid.

I said nothing, and moved the sandwich to the right.

"I would have come by earlier," she continued, "but Frau Hofflinger knocked on the door. She wasn't asking for the rent, though. She was taking up a collection for our soldiers stationed in Poland. She stayed quite a while, talking about how these were going to be such happy holidays." Smiling, Gerda placed a wedge of Münster on the folder.

"Stop putting things there," I said sharply. "That's not your tablecloth. You can see it's official business."

She looked at me, wounded. Whatever confidence she might have felt dissolved. "I'm sorry."

I picked up the file, wiped it off. "I think you'd better leave, Gerda."

She bent to kiss my forehead. Then she lifted her head, just the slightest, and looked toward the front desk, as if to see if she was being observed. I pulled away. "I'll be at home at the usual time." And flipping open the folder, I pretended to read.

"Commander Terskan," I heard her say on the way out.

"Tomorrow—remember." Rolf Terskan's voice came as a low rumble just before the door shut.

The letters *G T N* were stamped in red at the top of the page. That's all I saw. The confession was typed below; it was the block upon which, in three days, believing in his own sentence or not, a man would lay his head.

I looked over at Terskan. He was turned from me, facing the window that fronted onto the street. The brown cloth of his shirt barely moved as he breathed. He must have sensed my eyes on him, because he swiveled around.

I shoved the prisoner's file away. "At least the death is quick, isn't it?"

"You believe that, too?" said Terskan, understanding immediately. "That's only the lie." He sat back in his chair. "There is a process—as there is with everything. First, there's waiting to be caught—whether you want to be or not; then being arrested; then there's the imprisonment before the trial; the trial—you sit and listen to the sentence. Then there's another prison, usually in a different place. After that, you go to the room beneath this floor." He paused. "No, it's rare, Torgood, if any death in life is quick."

He turned back to the front window. He leaned closer in to the pane, watching.

After a moment, he went outside and a few minutes later came back with something pressed in his hand. "Gerda's glove," he said, shutting the door. "You'll want to take it back."

Each time I touched the cool empty leather neatly folded in my pocket, I felt soothed. It was the only safe comfort I had in the station. But when I arrived home and saw how Gerda looked at me, her mouth set in a straight line, still angry about how I'd treated her earlier, I didn't admit to having the glove. If I did that, I'd be talking, and I didn't know what else I might start to say. That I was going to be a witness to too much? That I hoped she'd put my new job out of her mind so she could touch me each day when I came home?

I told her the edge of the truth, that I was tired. And that I had no stomach for dinner. And that I was going to bed. Later, when she came in, I appeared to be asleep but for hours I lay listening to how lightly she breathed. Before the sun hit the crossbars of the window, I slipped from the warm sheets into my clothes. Not long after, I was down in the station's basement. There, I measured a man's head with a beige cotton tape, recorded the dimensions and asked him to please step on the scale. He did as I asked, but refused to speak even one word to me. Then I watched him walk from the room. Fewer than five minutes later, the guards brought back a body and placed it on the scale and I weighed that. The head was weighed separately. I also recorded where, on the length of the neck, the blade had done its work. At the end of the day, I took home our blue pot. Rolf Terskan, good to his promise, had washed and shined it. In it, too, he'd placed a small geranium with vibrant pink blooms. Its petals were perfect, like a baby's fingernails. Gerda was thrilled when she saw it. How thoughtful he is. Be sure to thank him for me, she urged. I said I would, but as for now, I had nothing I wanted to say. I was much too tired. The next morning, when Terskan informed me that two more be-headings were scheduled for Monday, he patted my back very gently; it was the same way Gerda's hands had patted the new cutting into its dark circle of soil, with just enough pressure for the shallow roots to grab hold.

Before and after each "body recording," as we referred to it, Terskan would walk over to my desk. Before he'd trimmed my hair, now he smoothed the brown shirt over my shoulders. "Well-ironed," he'd say. Or: "You'll need another one soon, won't you?" Then, he'd pause and ask in a somber way: "Ready?" Knowing the question was coming, knowing it signaled I'd go below while he'd stay above at his desk, I came to dread the solicitude. His rituals only extended the tension. They became part of the elaborate procedures in which, in the bright basement, I played a part.

"Done?" I'd hear as I climbed back up the stairs. "There's a glass of water on your desk. Take your time. Last week, if I'm correct, you spilled it and only made more work for yourself. Or did you leave the retyping for Prudmann, to give him something to do?"

On the day I took the body measurements of Ruthe Kauss, I couldn't bring myself to go home. In the month I'd been at the task, she was the first female I'd had to hold a tape to. I felt unmanned, emotional, a dressmaker going about on trembling knees, wanting to clothe, not strip her body. The perversion of this, of the thinness of her frame and the violation it was soon to undergo, unnerved me all the more. When the condemned were men, I could at least try to erase myself; but here, where the difference between the two of us was all the more marked, where it was clear I was to live and she, already weak, was to be made even worse off, I could hardly bear my own shame. The records said she was thirty-two years old; a teacher of literature for grades ten through twelve.

I said, "Please step on the scale, gnädige Frau."

She didn't move.

Fixing the paper under the metal pincer of my clipboard, I said, "Please, on the scale." I let go of the pincer and it snapped down. I glanced over at her. She was no longer wearing the shoes she'd been assigned and her stockings were off. Her feet were reddened and small—so many small bones.

She said in a shaking voice, "No, I won't do what you say."

"Please, up." I pointed the pencil toward the scale.

Incredibly she said again, "No. I told you—I won't." She started to cry.

Eikenhorn was guarding the door and he called to Kremmetz, who was waiting out in the hallway. The two of them lifted her by her elbows.

I finished the job—all of its stages; then I went outside behind the station. Band music floated cheerfully through the air. I sat with my back to the wall that harbored the heat stove and, though it was cold November, slept.

Terskan must have seen me; certainly someone took that blanket from one of the cells and doubled it over me. I had dreams only of the backs of people, dreams of coats flapping and blowing away in a gust. Or maybe they weren't phantasms at all and what I absorbed was true: vagrants, their chins tucked well into their collars, cursing at me as they passed as quickly as possible through this, the well-swept alley of the police.

When I got home, the lights were out. I pushed open the hall door and, through the dimness, saw the bed. Gerda had the sheets up to her chin, the linens ghostly against the thin curves of her cheekbones and fingers.

"Torgood?" Her whisper mixed fear and certainty.

"Yes." I unbuttoned my shirt and threw it on the chair, then I kicked off my shoes.

"It's so late, even later than last night. I left some soup out. Did you eat?"

Half-clothed, I sank onto the covers. "No."

She propped herself up on one elbow. Her teeth were bared; she was smiling. "Everything is still all right, isn't it?"

I shut my eyes. "Yes, fine. Don't worry."

"Aren't you going to wash and come to bed?"

"I am in bed."

"You're like this again. I can't stand it."

I wanted to shout at her—but what had she done? She'd done nothing.

The mattress shifted a bit, then she slid her half of the covers over me and began to tuck the blanket tightly around my shoulders.

I pushed her hands away. "Stop it. You need all this swaddling, I don't. Leave me alone."

"I thought you were cold."

"You don't know what I am."

She was silent. She got out of bed. "I'll get you your dinner. At least I'm used to doing that by now." She threw a sweater on over her nightgown.

I followed her to the kitchen. She'd turned the small table lamp on, and draped a blue cloth over it. The glow extended only so far; most of the room was in shadow. In the center of the table, with its three heads of blooms turned nearly purple, was the pink geranium. I stood in the doorway for a second. Then I pulled out my chair and sat down.

She took the lid off the soup pot and dipped in the ladle. There was something in that sound, in the slight suck as the metal broke the liquid surface and the broth was pulled down into the smaller bowl, that made me want to draw Gerda to me and cry. That small sob called up all I had locked inside. But she was so far away. "Gerda." I cleared my throat. "I have a surprise for you."

"You do?" Her voice actually lifted. "What?"

I pulled her glove out of my back pocket and held it up by its thumb, upside down. "Aren't you missing this?"

Her eyes widened. "You have it? Where did you find it?"

"I didn't find it." Then I heard myself say: "I don't know who did. But it was brought to the station, and here it is."

"After all this time," she murmured. "Most likely some poor person was trying to decide whether or not to use it forever. Well, now I don't have to get through the winter wearing my old gloves." She turned back to the counter. "I'm glad to have it back. I promise I won't lose it again."

Reluctantly, I let it go.

"Maybe everything does return to us," said Gerda, placing a bowl of potato soup before me. "Who knows?"

I looked up and she smiled tentatively, touching her fingers to the nape of my neck.

"Your hair is long. I'm so glad he hasn't had to trim it again." She paused. "I want you to take Commander Terskan a little gift. I didn't tell you, but I made him something. It's not much, but since he's not expecting it, well, you know how he is. He thinks he knows everything about everything. That's why these little surprises mean so much to him."

I turned around in my chair. She stood at the sideboard, holding a folded white dishtowel.

"What? That?"

"I know it might look silly," she said, embarrassed. "But I kept thinking about what he told me, about cleaning up after himself. I know he'll like using this. I embroidered the edges in two colors. And it's clean. I washed it twice."

"Terskan doesn't want your dishtowel."

"I worked on it," she said, her chin jutting out. "He will."

I stiffened. "Well, I'm not giving it to him. You think that these little things, the soup, and this bit of cloth, mean anything anywhere? You have no idea. You really don't. Do you want to hear what I do now? Why I hate coming home? Why Terskan doesn't bother anymore to cut my hair? A dishtowel. You want to give him a prettied little rag. Unbelievable."

"How do you know what he wants?" She snapped the cloth at my head. "Be quiet!"

The edge of the cloth hit just under my left eye. Without a word, I turned around. As I did, I heard her footsteps going to the back of the house. She should have come near; she should have leaned over and whispered: No, tell me—tell me. I won't let us go on this way. I know what it is—oh, I have from the first. But you must tell me, too.

You must tell me, too. That was the other side of it—I had to tell, just as she had to ask. But as the bedroom door clicked shut and I sat methodically spooning that bland white soup up to my lips, I knew that neither one of us would turn now. Neither wanted to bear hearing the other speak. For once we began it, we wouldn't be who we wanted to believe that we were. We'd be these two, instead. This man whose fingers held the tapes, this woman whose fingers didn't quite open to his in the dark. These two people with eyes both staring and shut.

And knowing it, that this was who we were, that we were no longer who we had been, those who were innocent, who were sweetened by what they held on to, at that moment, I actually ached for the blade's falling slice. I wanted it to end the life between us, to cut the tissue of our marriage so cleanly that our bodies would fall away, separate, and finally lie still. But Terskan was right about that: the blade, primed, doesn't fall fast—that's just the lie. Instead, I understood, there would be only this tiny, day-by-day gnawing, with a burrowing animal's small, though sharp enough teeth. Turning and turning it over in little dirty paws. Holding on to it as it got smaller and smaller and smaller.

The next morning Gerda was tight-lipped and angry. I got out of bed and instead of rising with me, she turned away; she wouldn't speak to me. Secretly, I was glad; now she carried the blame for the silence between us. I dressed, drank some ersatz coffee, filled a sack with some lunch, and, though it was much too early—barely a quarter past five—I left.

The wind had a chill to it. I tried walking around the

still-dark streets, under the party banners flapping from the buildings in silent enthusiasm, but I only became more anxious. Phrases from our fight kept coming back to me. Finally, I headed for the station. As soon as I walked through its green doors all the tension flooded out of my body. I felt loose-limbed, clear-headed, as if I'd downed a shot of schnapps. Everything around me looked so predictable and orderly, I felt like whistling.

Near the back, Commander Gruber, Terskan's night replacement, stood over the sink, splashing water onto his face. He gave me a sidelong glance, his eyes a blotchy red. "Water's too cold," he said, shaking his head. "I never take the time to heat it."

"Well, you'd have to go downstairs for that, Commander— to use the stove."

"No need," he said, shaking his squarish head from side to side. Drops of water sprayed against the wall. "Rather take it like a man. More bracing, yes?"

I sat back in my chair and looked around as if I'd never been in the station before. The ceiling lights were burning; pools of light lay over everything. "Is it always this peaceful? Maybe I should clerk at night."

"Well, it won't get you off the day shift." He reached for a limp towel. "We have our orders. That's true for everyone."

"Is it?" I mused, a bit too familiarly. "Given the stack of papers on my desk these past few mornings, it doesn't look as if Prudmann has been reporting in at night."

Gruber straightened up. "Yes, well," he said. "That's a sad state of affairs. His wife is in the hospital. He's afraid she's slipping away and, from what I hear, he's probably right." He paused. "He wanted to stay with her. I told him he could."

"Yes," I said, in just the matter-of-fact tone Terskan used.

"I thought you must have told him that." With a twinge of pleasure, I watched the furrow deepen between Gruber's eyebrows. "Of course he wasn't disobeying orders on his own."

The night commander rubbed his chin with his sleeve. "I'll check about the shift," he said.

"Good." Suddenly tired, I put my head down on my arms and a while later I heard Rolf Terskan come in; his boots were loud against the floorboards.

"Torgood? I thought you slept enough yesterday."

I raised my head and sat up.

He was shrugging off his winter overcoat. "Perhaps you should be at home. You're not due in yet. What's wrong?"

"I'm fine, Commander Terskan."

"You don't look fine. To be blunt, you haven't for some time." He put a cardboard box down on my desk. Untying it, he lifted out a dark-chocolate dobos torte.

"What's that?"

"A gift." He placed the cake carefully on my blotter. "Take it home with you."

Gruber came over. "He wants to clerk at night for me."

"Absolutely not," said Terskan. "Call in one of the regular patrolmen if you need companionship."

"I didn't say I needed companionship," Gruber protested. "I said Stella asked to clerk at night for me."

"I oversee his work, Walter. His job has already expanded in its responsibilities."

"I heard about that, yes," Gruber said slowly. His forehead creased. "Maybe he should go home at night, you're right."

"Commander Terskan, I asked to come in." I began to get up.

"No." His hand dropped onto my shoulder. "You're shirking your duty. A wife needs her husband. As for this beautiful seven-layer cake, I won it in a bet with the head chef at

Kaski's. Take it, with my compliments. I'm sure Gerda will be pleased. People need luxury when things are hard."

I stiffened. "Thank you, but you've already done enough for us."

"Don't be silly. It's a gift, Torgood."

"You know I can't reciprocate, Commander Terskan. I'll always be in your debt."

"Not in the least! Don't worry about me, I know how to bet, I won't starve. I'll have another sweet in no time."

"Will you be quiet," I growled. "I said, no. I told you I won't take your stinking gifts."

"Now, just a moment, now," Gruber sputtered.

"Walter." Terskan tightened his grip on my shoulder. "I'm in charge here. Leave."

I struggled to rise under his hand. "I'm sorry, Commander."

He gazed down at me with steady eyes. "It's not simply a bad lung that makes you like this, is it? If you won't go home as I suggest, go to a back cell and lie down. Better, go downstairs. Go to a cell in the basement—there's one empty now. I just want you out of my way."

"What?" I sank back into the chair. "Commander Terskan?"

The skin under his chin was flushed a raw red. "I gave you an order, clerk Stella. Are you refusing me?"

"No." I barely got the word out. I stood unsteadily, pushed the chair away.

Gently, as he used to when he still gave me the haircuts, he rubbed the nape of my neck.

"I'm sorry, Commander Terskan. Believe me."

He nodded. "You can stay up here at your desk. You've told me what I needed to know. The trial's over."

He turned his back. "I have some business to clean up, but when I come back, I expect you to be following routine.

Don't make me put you down among the traitors." He seized his coat and, shoving his arms through the sleeves as he walked, left. The door shut.

I couldn't seem to move. Except for a prostitute in a back cell, there was no one else in the station. There was no one downstairs either—no one I knew about—living out the day next to the guillotine. It was morning, still early. I could hear Terskan whistling. I could tell just how far along the road he was.

Quickly I crossed over to the main desk, the one he and Gruber shared. I took the key from beneath the ashtray and unlocked the middle drawer, the one from which he had taken that envelope with my change of orders. Two pencils went rolling to the back. Empty. The two side drawers, then. The first opened without the key. On top, folded in thirds to cover from one edge to the other, was a copy of the town paper. I glanced at it. Worthless. Under it was a sheaf of letters. *Commander Terskan, This is to confirm* . . . the top one said. I picked up the pile. The next: *Commander Terskan, We notify you that* . . . No, nothing. *Commander Terskan, Be advised as of your receipt of this letter* . . . *Commander Gruber* . . . What was that doing here? I licked my thumb, flipped letter over letter. *Commander Terskan* . . . *Commander Terskan* . . .

It took no more than a minute, perhaps less. . . . *We have approved your suggestion that such measurements might prove useful. As you point out, even the slightest fact can have impact when applied in the correct scientific manner. We will advise the appropriate personnel when our forms are complete. Certainly, we value your ongoing contributions* . . .

My hands began to tremble. I skimmed the document again. But it showed the same facts.

Rolf Terskan had brought all this upon me. For what? For

his good standing in the eyes of some distant judges? A secure place for himself, could that be true?

The bulkhead creaked at the back of the building. I heard footsteps going into the basement. I slid the letter back into the pile and hurriedly shut the drawer, relocked the middle one. By mistake, I almost pocketed the key, but it too went back where it belonged. From below, in a man's clear voice came the shout: "No, I refuse—I refuse to do it!" Then I heard the cell door slam and a surge of laughter.

I went back to my desk. Terskan didn't return. Instead, he sent word he'd be at home the rest of the day, and into the night, too. I kept working in a kind of agitated haze. When it was not quite dinnertime, Gruber appeared, shaking the wind from his muffler.

He turned around, his face blistered by the cold. "Awful. Winter." He sat down gracelessly at the main desk and pulled out one of the side drawers.

I watched him reach in.

"You can leave," he said, and took out a pencil.

"Commander Gruber—?" I stopped, not knowing what next to say.

"Prudmann will be in tonight," he said sharply. "No need for you to stay, even if you wanted to. Go home."

"What?" The good news shook me as much as if it were my own. "His wife is better? She's recovered?"

"Probably not," he said, "but he's coming in. Too many people seemed to know that he wasn't working." He looked at me. "Well, I'll be glad for the company, even if he has a rough time of it."

My face flushed; I looked away. "Here, give him this, would you?" I pushed the layer cake across the desktop.

Gruber's eyes glistened as he grinned at me. "That's very kind. I certainly won't let anyone else know about it. I'll pass it on to him. I'm sure Prudmann and his wife will appreciate your generosity."

I felt sick to my stomach.

"Maybe I'll get a slice, too," he continued, gazing over at it. "Iced. And with all those layers. He's a real master, isn't he? No one can get these things anymore. There's just not enough, is there? Not enough of anything sweet to go around."

As soon as I turned the corner from the station, I broke into a run. But at Kempener, sawhorses blocked off the end of the street and a crowd had gathered. The Citizens' Band was holding a concert for the army's holiday fund. With a nod of permission from the bandleader, the audience began clapping in time to a popular drinking song. Some people started singing, but instead of the chorus: *We lift high our mugs, yes! Empty them now!* they sang with much laughter: *We lift high the Poles, yes! Show them who's won!* It would take too long to get through the crowd. I cut across to Grubenplatz, then through the empty vegetable market. Finally, I reached my corner of Ludwigstrasse. The exultant booming of the band's bass drums carried even that far.

Gerda had the lamp on in the front window, though the parlor beyond it looked dark. I fumbled with the lock at the door. Surely, she heard how much trouble I was having opening it. I put the key in again, pushed harder.

I was standing in the hall. "Gerda, where are you?"

"Here." Her voice floated happily toward me from the kitchen.

My heart leapt. I could hear the forgiveness and love in her voice. We would talk. I should have insisted last night; I should have begun it well before that. No matter. I would explain now what I'd seen and she would ask me, please, to clarify: How did he think he could get away with all this? What are we going to do, now that we know? Tell me. Ask me. Hurrying down the hallway, I seemed to shed my guilt over the past months as easily as I shed my coat. "Gerda!"

But the kitchen was quiet. From the two pots on the stove rose twin columns of steam, but there was no smell of food in the air. I walked over to the burners. There was only water in the pots, bubbling emptily away.

She came in from the bedroom, carrying a large, unwieldy box wrapped in the kind of patterned paper that used to be available before the war. She put it down on the table; it covered a good half of it. "This just came. You've made me so happy. I was waiting to unwrap it until you came home. Now I don't have to hold myself back any longer."

"What is it?"

Her eyes went cold. "You mean it's not from you?"

Mutely, I shook my head.

"Well, then," she said. She turned a little away from me, blocking my view, and ripped the paper along the seam. "Oh," she exhaled, the word mingled in her breath. "Oh, I never could have imagined."

"What?"

"The beauty of fur." Her back straightened and she didn't turn around. She put the round hat on her head, over her ears, and the stole about her shoulders. The stole was so thick, her narrow shoulders seemed twice their breadth as they joined up with the plush of the hat. She whirled around. The tips of the brown fur glistened and her eyes, too, looked exceptionally bright, her cheeks ruddy. It was as if Gerda weren't standing opposite me in our kitchen but was suddenly outside, poised at the edge of something vast, facing a brisk wind. She saw what it was that was coming toward her. Her mouth dropped partway open, then she laughed. "I can't wait to show him."

She left the kitchen door ajar. To preserve the heat of what little coal burned in the grate, I closed it not long after. I went to bed, and awoke, alone. That day, and the next, and the next, Rolf Terskan didn't come into the station. I received my transfer to Passau, the last town near the eastern border, on the fourth morning. It was just as well, given what I knew. I knew everything.

I traveled lightly, with only my clothes. I reported to Commander Friedrich exactly on time. His clerk showed me what to do to assist him. They had no guillotine in Passau, though the laws were still the laws and traitors were still subject to the full extent of them.

Questionnaire 1

Case no. ....

    Name of Institution: ....

    in: ....

First and family name of patient: .... maiden name: ....

Date of birth:......... City: .... District: ....

Last residence:......................... District: ....

Unmarr., marr., wid., div.: Relig:.. Race[a] .... Natlty: ....

Address of nearest relative: ....

....

Regular visits and by whom (address): ....

....

Guardian or Care-Giver (name, address): ....

....

Cost-bearer:.... How long in this inst.: ....

In other Institutions, when and how long: ....

How long sick:.. From where and when transferred: ....

Twin $^{yes}_{no}$ ... Mentally ill blood relatives: ....

Diagnosis: ....

....

Primary symptoms: ....

....

Mainly bedridden? $^{yes}_{no}$... Very restless? $^{yes}_{no}$..... Confined? $^{yes}_{no}$ ....

Incurable phys. illness: $^{yes}_{no}$ ..... War casualty: $^{yes}_{no}$ ....

    For schizophrenia: Recent case ...... Final stage .. good remission ...

    For retardation: Debility: .... Imbecile:.... Idiot: ....

    For epilepsy: Psych. changes .... Average freq. of attacks ....

    For senile disorders: Very confused .... Soils self ....

Therapy (Insulin, Cardiazol, Malaria, Salvarsan, etc.): Lasting effect: $^{yes}_{no}$ ......

Referred on the basis of §51, §42b Crim. Code, etc. .... By ....

Crime:... Earlier criminal acts: ....

Type of Occupation: (Most exact description of work and *productivity,* e.g. Fieldwork, does not do much.—Locksmith's shop, good skilled worker.—No vague answers, such as housework, rather precise: cleaning room, etc. Always indicate also, whether constantly, frequently or only occasionally occupied)

....

....

Release expected soon:...

[a]German or related blood (German-blooded), Jew, Jewish *Mischling* [half-breed] 1st or 2nd degree, Negro *(Mischling),* Gypsy *(Mischling),* etc.

The Stroke

In 1939, in 45 words on a sheet of personal stationery, Hitler issued a statement to leaders in the medical community: Aktion T4. Doctors were to select those patients who were infirm, insane, crippled, or in other ways "useless eaters" and "grant [them] release." Release, for the youngest, would come via lethal injection, for those older, by entering the first, experimental gas chambers. Of course, the patients—some 70,000—didn't know their fate. Patients rarely do.

WITH A STROKE, so much is lost. For the one who has the stroke, almost everything changes. The body acts up, is governed not by the mind but by its own dark mass. The sweetest face twitches, the most supple arm will not bend, the bowels obey gravity and flood out. And just as bad as the body is the mind.

"Awake?" A face peered around the white sheeting surrounding my bed. An old face, but round as a babe's and almost as hairless. Everything about it soft, except for something in the eyes. Apprehension, not quite hidden.

"Husband," I said. "Karl?"

He broke into a grin. "Correct, Trude Prudmann." He slipped through the opening. Against his wool greatcoat he clutched a brown cardboard file box. He wasn't a tall man.

When he leaned over the box to kiss me, his skin smelled cold, like the wind.

Hungrily, I placed my palms against his reddened cheeks. "I woke up last night only once. Or maybe just twice."

"Good! The more you sleep, the sooner you'll get well."

"Did you have trouble, Karl?"

"Trouble?" He withdrew first one arm then the other from his coat. "Why ask that?"

"Because trouble"—stuttering, I searched for the rest of the thought—"if there's trouble at Kreiswald station. At the police work. Did you have some?"

He shrugged. On his brown shirt, the epaulets arched up like cats, then slowly slid down and relaxed. Wasn't that how he answered my questions at home, with a shrug? I would be in the kitchen, yes, hear the door open, then footsteps coming in to where I was, to where I had the food laid out—hot and filling, a breakfast that was more like a dinner. There would be stew and bread, a big pot of ersatz coffee. Karl, after the night always spent hard at work, he answered in this very way, didn't he?

"I hope you're listening to me, Trude. I just said, here's a surprise."

I looked over.

In his hands was a cake, a magnificent dobos torte, frosted in chocolate. Above it was his happy face. He said: "A gift from one Torgood Stella."

"Closer," I ordered.

Karl told me something more, but I didn't hear it. Words can be nonsense. There, right in the dark cake, a slice was missing. I couldn't take my eyes from the wedge—made completely of air. I struggled to my elbows to peer down inside it. Was it illness that made me respond only to what was gone? "Is this really from Torgood Stella?" I said. "Who is he?"

Karl laughed. "The day clerk. And you're right, it can't be from him." Bending again, he whispered, "I think Commander Gruber paid Stella with a piece of this for pretending it was from him. Gruber knows about our troubles. But he dislikes drawing attention to himself—that's why all the subterfuge." Karl lowered the cake into the box. Stamped on the box were the words *Intake Files*, with a line drawn through them. Below that, inked in small blue letters I could make out: *R. Terskan/winnings*. "Trude, do you remember Commander Gruber?"

My eye was twitching. I didn't answer.

"Walter Gruber's my superior. A big, heavy man. He's the one who gave me the leave. Yesterday, though, he called me in. He said people have noticed my absence—illness in the family or not. I have to report for my shift from now on." Karl bit his lip. After a pause he said, "But the cake is for you. I am giving his gift to you."

"But Doctor Gruber wants me on a strict diet."

"You need to say Traub," he said quietly. "Doctor Traub. Gruber's my superior."

"Well, any food not on his list can trigger a new seizure."

"That's wonderful, Trude."

I stared at him.

"See, you remembered what the doctor said, that's wonderful. And as for the cake, diet or not, it's yours." He drew over the visitor's chair and sat down, beaming. "What do you plan to do with it?"

"Something, Karl."

"Should I find out if it's on the approved list?"

"No. Give it away." The words leapt from my mouth. "I want to—I'll give it to the children's group."

"What children's group?"

Excited, I jerked my chin toward the curtain's opening. "The one here."

"But this is a rest home," he said, "a convalescent home for adults. The children have their own hospital in the center of town. Do you want me to take this to Kinderschloss?"

"But the children are here, Karl. I know about it."

"I'm sure you're mistaken."

I shook my head. "They hide. People hide them here."

"You're not talking about a locked ward?" There was a scraping sound as he shifted in the chair. "A while back I heard something at the station about some kind of new program for the hospitals. I thought it was just talk." He gazed at me in dismay. "No, you must be mistaken, because I would have filed a copy of the order. The police are always notified of a change in the government's programs. Besides, you haven't been out of your bed even once—how could you know about this?"

"How worried!" I chided. "You think I'm making everything up. But sometime, in the middle of a night, there were children rushing down the hallway. It was late and, oh, I just have to laugh, thinking of it! They were babbling and singing such silly things. At first I thought I was being awakened by angels."

He leaned forward. A single strand of grey-blond hair fell across his forehead. "Listen to me, if they *are* here, those children are being isolated for their own good. It's not unlike, for example, people who are put in protective custody, at the station. You know, where I work. Even I can't see certain prisoners. But it's for a good reason."

"No, these are only sick children."

"And you're sick, too," he said. He sat up, his back hard against the chair. From the white metal tray, he took hold of my water glass. As he drank the liquid down, his throat moved in three great gulps.

I laughed—it looked like he was singing. "Remind me again, Karl, the tunes of some nursery songs?"

The glass clinked down, empty. "Trude—"

"It's awful to forget something that simple. Please."

He shut his eyes and under his breath sang, "One pfennig, two pfennig, give me three for these peppercorns."

"Yes, that is one." My head rolled a little to the side. "I'll sing it with them and then—this cake. Can't you see how they would like it? I can manage a wheelchair, if someone will push me."

He grimaced. "You're still so weak. We have to think about Doctor Traub. Doesn't he want you to rest? He wants you to get well."

"I remember another song!"

"You do?"

I hung on to the edge of the bed. "Is there one with a last line that goes: 'Yes, yes, here's three bags full.' "

He squinted into the distance. "There is, I think. But I can't recall any more of it."

"Try," I urged. "What's the one that ends"—I gathered my breath and sang out—" 'three bags *full!*' "

He broke into a laugh. "I can't remember, I swear!"

From the other side of the room came a moan.

Karl stood quickly. He called into the sheeting, "Do you need help?"

"Be quiet." A woman's voice—thin, without any depth. "I'm not well and can't sleep with such noise. I'm going to summon the nurse."

The back of Karl's neck turned red. "I'm very sorry, gnädige Frau. We forgot ourselves. It won't happen again."

He sat down heavily. I reached for his hand. The wind was off him. His skin was warm, like mine. "I want to see them," I whispered. "I haven't seen anything young and fresh since I came here."

He shook his head. "This wouldn't be happening if Ruthe or Alex were here. Ruthe, certainly, could be spared for a few days." The words were furious under his breath. "This warrants a hardship leave. I know it does."

"You're angry with me?"

He stopped and his eyes searched my face. "Do you know who I'm talking about?"

"They are our children," I murmured. Ruthe, born August 9, 1921. Alex: June 16, 1918.

"You remember them." He kissed my forehead. Karl's lips were always soft, yes.

My daughter: brown hair, blue eyes, big smile. "Oh, Mamma!" she'd always say, laughing. "Oh, Mamma, why?" On a state work detail for girls—a farm east of Munich. My son: nice, like Karl, but called up also—in the army medical corps, student division. One out the door one day, then with the next day the other gone, too.

"And this war." I turned my face, as if slapped. "I remember it. Of course I remember! Why can't you let me see these little ones?" I spoke with such force, spittle dribbled over my lips. "Don't you understand what I want?"

Karl reached over and brushed the tip of his index finger to my chin. A clear string of spittle came away with it. He looked around. "That towel, please."

Awkwardly, I pushed it across the blanket.

"Thank you." He put his dried hand in his lap. He looked down and away from me, silent.

After a while I said, "I want to see a child. A real one."

He seemed to shrivel and pull into himself.

"Karl?"

Finally, he looked up. "It's a beautiful cake." He reached over for me. "Give it away."

I was dozing. Doctor Traub pushed aside the sheeting. With one step, he commanded the space. The white coat, the stethescope and clipboard, the way his elbows were held in close at his sides—he looked not burdened but elegant. He saw the box at the end of my bed and immediately put his dry, graceful fingers on it. He gave the cardboard a slight prod.

"What is this?" His voice was light, accusatory, the same tone he used when a muscle twitched on the right side of my face.

"I need your permission for it," I said.

He studied me. "Oh? I received a note from your husband this morning, saying he must speak with me as soon as possible, but I have no idea why. Is this what he wanted?"

I smiled, gave a quick nod. "Yes. To let me go to the children, here, and give them this cake."

The corners of his mouth turned up. "This is a cake?" The word sounded suddenly moist.

"It's a gift, a dobos torte."

"You wouldn't mind?" he said, laying down his clipboard. "May I see it?"

I nodded.

"Butter and sugar. Eggs." Reciting, he lifted the lid. "Flour, vanilla, baking powder, chocolate." He looked up at me. "You have eaten a piece."

"I didn't."

He glared, his eyes very blue. "You don't remember. Obviously, you can't. You were to eat only what I prescribed. Don't you want to get well? Someone used up all these ration coupons—unheard of these days—mistakenly thinking to give you a special treat and now you've harmed yourself."

"No, Doctor."

"No? What is this, then, this vacancy?"

I stuttered, "It was given to me that way."

"Who gives a cake that's already eaten?"

"I can't remember the name. A man who works for my husband. At the police station."

"That can't be." Doctor Traub took a deep breath. "Your husband is a clerk and no one works for him." He waited. "Do you remember that about your husband? That he's just a clerk?"

Ducking my head, I started to cry.

"So it must have been someone else. Who had access to these many coupons and why use them on you?"

I moaned, unable to answer. My sobbing took on a faster rhythm.

"Well," said Doctor Traub. He turned away and examined the box itself. Running his fingers across it, he bent down for a closer look. "Well," he said under his breath. He straightened back up. "Well, you mustn't let your weeping upset you, Frau Prudmann. Crying like this is a symptom of stroke victims. It isn't real. The tears are mindless, just useless." He laid a hand on my shoulder.

"But I want to get well."

"Then you will. It could be that your stroke is milder than I first thought. Of course, I'm speaking lightly, but at the worst, over time, you'll have to live with a few annoying blank spaces floating in and out." His hand lifted. He took a swipe at the curtain, which shuddered. "Quite soon, I'll be sending you away."

I caught my breath. "I'm getting better?" I said. "Then, you'll let me take the cake to the children?"

Doctor Traub laughed boyishly, in one loud splash. "So, she *can* hold on to a thought. This visit gets more and more surprising." He scribbled a few words on his clipboard and drew a mark further down on the page. "Nurse, bed number two!"

A nurse came around the sheets. The young one, with black hair, and dark, heavy-lidded eyes. A gypsy's face, yes— despite a starched white uniform, the dress and cap. She glanced my way, eyelids lowered, then said, "Doctor?"

"Our patient has expressed the desire to leave bed for the first time. What do you think of that?"

She hesitated. "It could be good, Doctor."

"I'll do just the routine examination." He took a tongue depressor out of his breast pocket and turned to me. "Open your mouth, please, Frau Prudmann."

In the next moment, the cold metal pressed down on my tongue.

"Open wider, and tilt your head back. I want to see the row above. Good.

"No gold." He dropped the instrument into a jar of alcohol the nurse held. "Mark it on the permanent file, please. We might as well have the information.

"There are metals," said Doctor Traub, facing me, "that react adversely with certain important medications, but you have no cause to worry. Now, once more, what was it you wanted from me?"

"To give the cake to the children."

"Fine." He wrote down a few more words. The pencil made a soothing sound. "Nurse, I have to examine just one more patient, then I'm going to get some sleep. The night's been very long and I don't want to risk an error in judgment."

He flipped over the sheet on his clipboard. "I want you to take this box over to the K-6 end-ward. Tell the head nurse to wait and give it only to those patients I've approved for release tonight—and then only to the ones who will know they're eating it. It might keep them quiet. If it works, let's remember something like it for the next time."

"But I want to see them," I cried out, stung.

"Certainly you may give away this cake to anyone you choose," he said with a tight smile, "but I can't allow you to enter the ward. These children are easily upset; you have no idea how to control them. They're like little horses. Like wild, long-legged colts butting each other, excited by sugar held out in the generous palm."

Without turning away—he didn't look down at what his hand was doing—he reached into the box. He skimmed a bit of the frosting off the cake. Slowly, he placed the dark coin on his tongue. Only barely did he close his mouth; he was letting the chocolate melt without pressing it down.

"Incredible," he murmured, closing his eyes. Standing in front of the bed like that he looked ill. All his concentration was directed inward. His eyelids fluttered, lashes dark against the coarse skin.

"Doctor?" the nurse ventured. "A wheelchair? Should I take the patient with me part of the way?"

He looked up, startled. "Of course." He swallowed the icing. "I want to know how she does, as a test of her stamina.

"After all," he said, bending quickly, fixing the lid on the box, "that's what we do here, we get you back on your feet. Nurse will push you, Frau Prudmann. You'll remain in the hallway while she delivers the cake. Just the hall, no further—then you return."

I was wheeled through the curtains. Something made me look back—just as people do when at some distance from a place they never thought they'd ever leave. Narrow; no more than a slot. Shocked, I jerked back around. And there—in front—was another patient. For the first time I saw someone else, one of the others who shared the room.

One of the curtains was tied back. Through the open wedge of the enclosure, I could see an old woman resting on her back. Maybe she'd broken a hip. There was a swollen, mummylike shape to the bottom half of her body, but the grey blanket covered everything. Doctor Traub was picking up his clipboard. "You haven't been out of this bed in how long is it now? Six weeks is it?"

"Longer," she said, the thin voice familiar. The one who yelled at my husband. "Eight."

The nurse pulled my shoulders back against the chair. "I hope you're not having trouble sitting forward," she said severely. "You wanted to do this so much."

She wheeled me through the maze of white sheeting and out to the hall. A nurse with a tray full of medicines hurried toward us. Just behind her came another nurse, pushing a young man on a gurney. The blanket wrapped around him had slipped; he was in an army uniform, not hospital garb. His arms, wound in gauze, hung down over the sides so that his blackened fingertips just missed brushing the tops of the wheels. He was groaning horribly.

"Expect more," this nurse whispered. She pushed him toward us at a slow pace. *Marta*, I learned from her—the gurney-nurse—was my nurse's name. She'd said: "We're getting them, Marta. They're coming in from the invasion."

"I thought Poland gave way."

"It did. Maybe this is from somewhere else. Maybe to the north," said the other one—she was passing, and finally she was behind—"Oh, good god, I need a bucket. He's spitting up."

I gripped the file box so it wouldn't shift on my lap. "There's so much activity out here."

We were turning the corner. The doors lining the hallway were all closed, each painted the same shade of green. From behind them came a few moans. I heard up close to my ear, "Your husband's the one who works for the police? I've seen him. He seems very devoted to you."

I nodded, looking about at the doors we were passing. "He's an important man. He has two men working for him. Gruber is one of the two. Gruber's a stellar clerk."

"Oh," she said. She patted my arm.

We were at the end of the hallway. "Well, let's rest right here, gnädige Frau."

I leaned forward. This door—green like the others—was different because it was metal-clad. I couldn't hear anything from inside.

"Since I won't be here to catch you," she said, coming around in front, "you'll have to sit back." She took two brown, wide cloth straps and wound them just under my ribs and around the chairback. Her hair, as she was securing the ties, brushed my face. How sweet she smelled, like flowers.

"You're set, aren't you? Now, you know I'll be gone for just a few moments?" She lifted the box from my lap.

"Don't do this to me, Marta."

She flushed. "What did you say?" Her whole face opened up and then shut. It was startling how quickly the stillness swept in. The surprise over, her face was as smooth as a mirror. Yes, a gypsy's talent for erasing her own surface. How did she get a racial purity certificate in order to work?

"I'm sorry," she said quietly. "Of course. Did you want a last look?" She bent over to show me the inside of the box. The dobos torte sat in it. One slice gone. Gouged across the top icing.

"I want to see them." My tongue moved thickly. "Just one moment, Marta, please."

She winced. "You can't." She snapped the box closed and stood up. She took a key from a hook to the right of the door jamb. She inserted it in the lock.

"I have orders from Doctor Traub," she declared, stepping inside. She wasn't talking to me but to someone in the ward. Behind her, in the door's open angle, I saw the side of a desk, a white skirt, and a thrust-forward, white-stockinged leg.

"Are those files in there?" a new voice sighed. "If they're

for tonight, I don't know how we're going to manage. He only examined twelve."

Marta was hidden from view; but her fingers were curled lightly around the edge of the door, not opening it further—but not closing it. Where were the children? I gripped the wheels of the chair and tried to go forward. I pushed the wrong way.

The other nurse—the one at the desk—said: "I thought we were set on a dozen being released. It was terrible Monday night, trying to get our twenty into the van. It was too crowded. You should have seen. Some wouldn't go in, scared to climb up into it. And the others, already inside, were trying to get out."

"I don't want to," a boy cried out, the words garbled. "I don't want to go to heaven." From the back, joining in, came other high cries and squeals.

"Shhh!" the desk nurse said. "What are you saying? You don't know. Everything is fine. You are lucky, lucky children."

The chair scraped back. "Well, what is it?" she asked. "Did they change the number being released tonight from your ward, is that it?"

Marta's fingers disappeared from the door's edge, sending the angle gliding open a bit wider. "It's not what you think, Rosa. Take a look inside." She stepped forward, to the desk.

I pushed the wheelchair a few centimeters. There, a little girl. She was sitting on the floor. Her back was to me. Such sweetness, to be that size, such small, thin shoulders. And down her back, the blond ends quivering just above the floor, a single, thick plait. I would have braided her two; one seemed much too heavy for such tiny shoulders. Her little head was trembling enough as it was. Clearly, she couldn't support its weight. Just then, her neck dipped and her head sank with the spasm to the side. Angled like that, she saw me.

Her eyes widened. With a huge smile, she slapped her hands on the floor. Rocking back and forth, she tried to get enough leverage to stand. Her knees were bent in front of her chest, but whenever she tried to get up on them, her feet slid out, one to each side. "Mamma," her voice was bell-clear. "Come!"

The desk nurse caught her breath. "Doctor Traub sent this?"

The door shut.

"He didn't leave a message with you?" Karl sat uneasily in the visitor's chair. "I don't understand why he didn't respond to my note. I checked at the front desk."

The quiet snoring in the room floated in from all different directions. It was like having cobwebs fall on my face. I waved my hand back and forth in the air. Terrible.

"I must speak with Traub," he continued, "but I can't get hold of him. When I'm working, he's on duty, too. Maybe Gruber will help us out one last time. Stella's been transferred—a slot's opened up on the day shift. I don't know Commander Terskan, but if Gruber agrees to talk to him on my behalf about Stella's position, then I can work days until—until you're home again. If you need anything, I want to be here. That's very important, that I take care of you. I have to tell Doctor Traub that, talk to him a little."

"All these names." I brought my arm down with a thud. "I don't know what you're talking about. I'm no good anymore, you should just leave."

"Don't say that," he urged. "Concentrate. You know, when I was looking for your doctor—that's Doctor Traub—a nurse came to speak with me."

"Don't bother with her name, I can't remember it."

"It's Marta." He paused. "Marta told me you gave the dobos torte away. I was surprised. I didn't think he would allow you to see a locked ward." Clearing his throat, he leaned forward. "How are you feeling?"

I shrugged.

"Marta told me that you sat up in the wheelchair the entire time, that you seemed alert and in control of yourself. She even said that afterward she wrote down on your chart how well you did. That's good news, a good report for your doctor. Do you remember any of that?"

I turned to the sheeting, my right eye furiously twitching.

"It's all right," he said.

"Why isn't there a window," I demanded. "Couldn't they have given me a window in here?"

Karl pressed my hand between his two. "What's important is that you've left your bed and brought back a good report. You can't let anything else bother you. This reaction is only because you've been trying so hard to get well. You've over-reached yourself."

"I'm not getting well." I pulled my hand away.

"Never say that, Trude, hear me? Not even to yourself."

I didn't respond.

"All right, now. Let's play our game, you like that."

"Do I? I don't know if I do."

"Let me start. All right? Are you watching?"

Karl closed his eyes. When he opened them, they looked a new shade of blue. He grinned. "Trude, I'm remembering something." And his hands, pudgy but not ungraceful, patted the air, slid down a bit and stroked, as if along a spine.

Despite myself, I smiled. "Our poor little Foo-foo."

He snorted. "Well, you didn't waste any time sparing my pride."

"Did you put her bowl outside for her, Karl?"

"I know how to feed a dog." Pretending indignation, he sat up straighter. "All right, your turn."

I fit my hands to the air and between my palms, something

took shape. Wider at the top than the bottom. A gentle curve. The two handles. I waited, then picked the swirled vase up by both handles, so as not to put the weight only on one. "I'm remembering something."

He guessed it. Then he wanted to show me the top of my bureau. "You'll be dusting it soon, very soon," he said, nodding. "Can you see the bureau, at home, what's on it? You always place these two objects just so." In the middle of the air, he drew two spidery shapes. At the ends of his fingers, I could see my comb, made of yellow ivory with a silver backbone, and my brush. It had a single blond hair snaking through the black bristles.

"A little girl," I said. "She saw me."

His hands dropped into his lap. "I wasn't drawing that."

"She saw me looking at her."

"But the nurse said you were left in the hall. She said you didn't go beyond the door. You couldn't have seen any of them in that ward."

"I saw her: she was trying to get up. That's right."

He was hesitant. "Well, good. Good for you. Did she like the cake, Trude? She must have been glad, a happy girl who made you happy in return."

"I think, yes. Yes, I think that happened."

"Then that's it," he said, "isn't it? That's it, sweetheart? You had a nice time. You were happy to come back and get a nice rest in your bed."

"No. She said something to me, but I wouldn't do it. I need to remember it. Why wouldn't I do it?"

"There's nothing more. You gave her the cake and she was happy."

"Something else."

"No, that's enough, really, it's good." said Karl, and kissed my forehead. He kept his lips on me for a long time. "You'll get better," he murmured into my skin. "I swear it." He pushed the chair back into the sheeting and stood up.

"What's wrong?" My heart started pounding.

"Nothing. I have to go to work."

"Not tonight. Tonight, stay."

"Trude, I'm still on the night shift. I don't have a choice."

"But I remember the other thing, about the girl. Don't go tonight and I'll tell you."

He said quietly, "Tell me."

I pursed my lips. I could think of nothing more. "Please stay, Karl," I said.

"I can't. Everything will be fine. I'm due at the police station at seventeen hundred. You know that, right?" He picked up his scarf, winding it twice about his neck.

I nodded.

He put on his coat, his cap. "Sleep and I'll be back in the morning, I promise. I'll have everything arranged then, a whole new schedule." He reached out and with both arms hugged the invisible shoulders rising to meet him. He even swayed to the side as if dancing. "I love you," he said. "I'll be back soon, don't forget."

I gave him another nod. As the sheets closed around him, swallowing him up, the muscles in the right side of my face seized. My jaw locked, halfway open. I was smiling; I couldn't stop. And crying, that too. The silent, saltless tears that didn't mean anything.

It was dark when I awoke, hospital dark. A faint light shone through the curtain. When I saw it, the relief that flooded through my body was enormous. The worst of my illness was over, that I had been told. The suffering was over; a new treatment would heal me and soon I would have all the old comforts. Hot food. Hot showers. Clean clothes. But they couldn't take everyone. It was just a short trip in a van. Didn't I want to go?

The light clicked off. My eyes adjusted to the darkness, to the long folds in the sheeting around my bed.

"Get her into the wheelchair," I heard a man whispering from the front of the room.

I lay very still.

"She needs to get her foot free first," whispered someone else. "It's tangled in the sheets. Lift your foot. Higher."

A woman moaned, "I can't."

Slowly, I covered my mouth.

There was a scuffling sound.

"Pick her up bodily."

"I'm an old woman, I don't bother anyone. I'm sure my daughter will come for me, if you'd only ask her."

"I've got her now." There was a thud.

"What are you afraid of? There will be children with you, too. A dozen."

"Children?"

"See how foolish you are to argue? You're a lucky, lucky woman."

"Take her out of here. Be quiet."

I heard a wheelchair creak.

"There's one more listed for release." A circle of light, the size of a fist, punched at my curtain, and slid away. A moment later there was a click. Darkness again.

Someone was walking across the room. The columns of my ghostly sheeting swayed to the right. This was a dream, an afterdream from a stroke. What in my brain was allowing this to happen? I could squeeze my eyes shut. I could open them.

A man whispered, "Here. Bring the gurney."

I shut my eyes.

The whine of a curtain being ripped back.

To my right, a woman groaned. All her words, muffled by the rustling sheets, were nonsense.

Something was rolled away.

After that, except for a loud, beating heart, it became very still. I lay in the dark. And when high voices filled the hallway with crying and laughing—scattering their sweet crumbs of sound—no one called out to me. Soon, again, it grew still. Far off, a door slammed. I wasn't to come.

The doctor stood by my bed. "Let's see how you are this morning." Picking up my wrist, he pressed a cool thumb against the vein, his eyes on his watch. "Too fast," he muttered, looking back up. I saw a flush spread, a mottled pink, under his chin.

"Don't do this," he said tersely. "You have to be well. I said you didn't require extreme intervention. Tell me. What's my name?"

Gruber?

"Think. Grab hold of it."

I looked at him. His face was drawn with concentration, showing me how to do this. "You're Traub," I said.

He nodded, smiling slightly. "And no more seizures, yes?"

I moved my lips, trying to untwist the sentence.

He was tapping his foot, impatient now.

"I don't know what time it is. What time is it? My husband promised to visit first thing, why hasn't he come?"

"I have to empty this room." He picked up his clipboard. "Do you remember what I just asked you about?"

"Seizures."

He nodded. "I want your answer. Yes or no?"

"Yes." I spoke slowly. "Yes, no more of them."

"Nurse!" he called.

It wasn't Marta who appeared but a pink-cheeked older woman, squat and stolid-looking.

"Take the patient down to the basement, to the showers, and help her wash."

"Wonderful, Doctor."

"She'll need a wheelchair. Get it, please." He turned to me. "Well, how do you like that," he asked pleasantly, passing the time. "You're leaving us."

With a little cry, I pressed the right side of my face against the pillow. "This morning? Now?" I could barely get the words out.

"Yes, now," he said sharply. "It's earlier than we might have released you in the past, but this isn't the past. There are soldiers coming in from the front all the time. We need to get them well as quickly as possible for our country's sake." He put his hand under my chin and turned my face toward him. "You'll have to convalesce on your own. Do you understand what I'm saying?"

"But where are you sending me?"

He gave me an incredulous look. "Home. Did you think I was sending you off for a month in the country?" He laughed in amazement.

"Oh, yes," he gasped, shaking his head, "there has to be someone who will thank me for this! Let me assure you, I don't know many clerks' wives who receive gifts of dobos tortes. But I know of even fewer who can take their sweet time convalescing."

He touched his fingers to his breast pocket. "Just try to remember, when your generous Commander Terskan asks, I was your doctor."

I passed through the maze with its white, fluttering angles. The nurse pushed me efficiently. Down in the basement, after the water of the shower fell in warm fat drops, drenching my skin and hair, she happily toweled me dry. She wheeled me up through the first floor hallway. It was different on this floor. Brighter. Some of the doors were propped open. I could hear conversations, even some laughter.

"Trude!" Karl came to a halt in the dead-center of the corridor. He was wide-eyed, still in his uniform, his greatcoat slapping back about his legs. "I tried to get here sooner, but I couldn't leave. After Gruber spoke to him, Terskan insisted on giving me a test to check my skills. And when I did get here and saw an empty bed, I thought—I thought they'd taken you, too. I know how such things work! I tried to reach Traub—"

"Your voice," said the nurse. "There are ill people here. You're in a hospital."

Karl shook all over, as if water had been tossed at him. "Correct." He pulled his shoulders back. "Forgive me. They just told me at the front desk—she's been given release. We're going home."

He took over from the nurse. He would bring the wheelchair back, give him one hour. He took off his coat, wrapped it about me. He put his policeman's cap on my head. Then I could smell him: the hair oil he used, his skin, the mustiness that came from the long night at the police station. "Karl?" I choked.

He squeezed my shoulder. "It's all right, it's fine. You're leaving." He pushed me quickly out the doors.

The wind was in my face. Invisible, it could erase anything. It did that, didn't it? Moved loose scraps about and set them down, finally, where they were supposed to be?

"I'll take you right in our front door," he was saying from behind. "Up the stairs, remember them? Twelve—twelve stairs. Up you'll go. The bedroom is where—to the left or the right?"

"Right?"

He laughed, and gave the chair an extra push. "Well, you'll see, soon enough. Soon, I'll put you between the sheets, make sure that everything around you makes you comfortable. I'll treat you"— he dropped his voice, whispered in my ear—*"like a queen."*

He pushed me down this street and that. Then he stopped. We were facing a brown brick rowhouse, a black door, two stories of narrow windows.

He left me on the stoop and went ahead. "Home," he said, shoving the door all the way open, "safe and sound."

I was looking down a dim, wallpapered hall. This, of all the places in the world, was mine. A touch of the floor under my feet would bring everything back, would make it all flood back. I wouldn't have to draw pictures in the air. A vase. A dog. (Where was the dog, tied in the back alley?) And on my bureau—an ivory comb and brush set?

My stomach lurched. The wheelchair tilted upward and I rode over the front step, into the hall. Further in, over a table, hung a photograph. I could hardly make out the two white faces, small as coins. "The children, wait!"

He was easing the wheelchair over the edge of the rug. "Not now, you have to get back into bed. It's been waiting for you, your half has been empty long enough."

We stopped at the base of the stairs. Karl came around and faced me, grinning nervously. He rubbed his palms against each other. "All right now, we do this together. Up on your feet." He slid an arm under my shoulders, hefted my weight up, into his side.

"Oh, Karl, stop."

"Better?" he said, gripping more tightly.

"It's not." My head flopped against his shoulder. "It's useless, look at me. I can't come back, not after everything. How can I?" I began to sob.

"You'll forget." His voice was rough with emotion. "You have to—forget about having a stroke, about these weeks in the hospital. I'll help you. You'll be healthy again, sooner than you know."

He took a breath. "Ready to go up? I'm ready. Ready?"

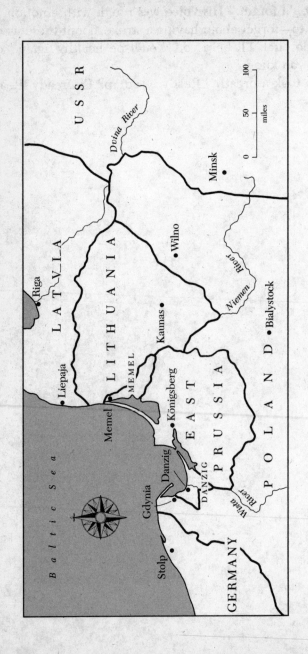

The Map

MAPMAKING WILL ALWAYS be profitable. You must remember how big the world is. For all its glories, the globe is quickly flattened, and flattened the dimensions shift. Sure, a man can make a good living by lifting one name from a land mass and carefully inscribing another, by flooding a new dye inside the freshened boundaries.

Even before the war, my work was in some demand. I'd been employed in Munich by the Schermer brothers, but on December 23, 1939, I was stopped by a sign on the building's front door: BUSINESS SUSPENDED UNTIL FURTHER NOTICE. In our huddled group, the bookkeeper Zweigler was the most distraught. She insisted all the ledgers were in order, that Stefan and Isaac had withdrawn no more funds than was usual, but when—after seeing the notice—she'd rushed to their houses, everything was quiet, locked up tight. She hadn't wanted to peek in the windows, but clearly the two brothers and their families were gone. Had they been picked up, as people could be these days, or had they taken it upon themselves finally to get out? She didn't know what to think.

Perhaps, she kept repeating as one by one we turned from the building, they'd only had some kind of emergency—might that be?—and just before the holidays?

I'd been waiting for this to happen from the first moment the new laws came into play. I couldn't believe that day was actually here. For five long years the Schermers had kept me working mostly on statistical maps, allowing me to work on the topographical jobs only when a project was running behind schedule. But now, at a fortunate time for me, I was on my own and I could choose the mix I wanted.

My first thought was to open a shop in Munich; then I reconsidered. Its neighborhoods were already studded with newspaper kiosks and leafleted lampposts—everywhere one looked there were pieces of paper appropriated for directing the populace. When a word, *Austria,* for example, first began to flicker from the headlines, the competition was fierce. Shoppers would sift through a man's wares, then: *Didn't he have the new version yet? This country* (and here they'd point to one of the shapes) *is ours.* The citizens of Munich knew where they stood and more importantly where others were to stand in relation to that. For fine art, they cared only somewhat; it was prompt correction they sought. A newspaper map, a cartoon of black and white, would do well enough. No, the more I thought about it, the more it seemed I needed to find some other place where I could make my mark.

After a process of elimination, I came up with three possibilities: Landau, Bensheim, and Kreiswald. In the end I settled on Kreiswald, a medium-sized city between Munich and Passau, for the sentimental reason that I'd camped near it on a scouting expedition when I was twelve or thirteen, some twenty years before. I remembered the surrounding woods as coniferous, dark green, valleyed, the hills as flowing up from a minor tributary of the Danube. Typical Bavarian topography. Of the town, I recalled not one brick. Still, it had to be some kind of a hub because the express trains stopped there; its name was superimposed above the long, delicately vertebral line that meant *railway* on the map.

At high speeds, you can't always see that it's snowing, but you can see the accumulation—a white cast over the ground. Only gradually, as you slow down for a destination, do flakes fill the air. I disembarked in a snowstorm, onto a bunting-draped platform crowded with soldiers and women. It was one of those shifting crowds a stranger can't get through because the people in it are trying to stay together until the last moment. A chorus of boys and girls wearing their Hitler Youth uniforms was grouped near the information board, singing folksongs, and some even smaller children stood about with tiny flags in their fists.

I made my way around the edges and out to the street where there was, at the intersection, a news kiosk. It was early evening, nearly dark. I picked up a copy of the local paper: *Finland Surrenders to Axis,* said the headline. Behind me, the whistle blew.

"But I just placed that notice," said the landlady almost angrily, peering through the pelting flakes. "I didn't expect someone to show up this quickly. In fact, I was hoping to wait until after the weekend."

"Are you telling me you have nothing to rent?"

With a sigh she stepped out onto the threshold, pulling the front door shut behind her—but not all the way. "No." She pushed a wave of thick brown hair off her forehead and gazed past me to the brick rowhouses that lined the street.

She was an unusual-looking woman, more a composite of individual features than one integrated vision. She had a heart-shaped face accentuated by a widow's peak in the exact center of her forehead, those cascades of brown hair, and a narrow, pointed chin. Her eyes were almost Oriental, but blue. Her mouth, like her eyes, looked foreign—too wide or maybe just too fleshy. She was slope-shouldered in the way women can get after forty or so, and although not especially short, because of the way she stood she came up only to my chin.

Shivering, she wrapped her arms under her breasts and said, "Those rooms weren't supposed to be vacant, you know."

My eyes dropped to the advertisement in the newspaper: *33 Ludwigstrasse. Three rooms, furnished, for immediate occupancy. 70 marks. Inquire: Hofflinger.*

"Frau Hofflinger, I need to find a place as quickly as possible. If you wouldn't mind, given the bad weather"—and here I handed her the *Kompass*—"would you tell me which of the listings is the nearest? Would it be this one, the third one from the top? Is that in this neighborhood?"

She took the newspaper but didn't so much as glance at it. "What is your name?"

"Felix Breslauer."

"Breslauer," she repeated and looked down at my bags. I had two suitcases, a small canvas duffle, a leather portfolio, and a paint box—all covered by a wet film of snow. The zipper on the art portfolio was so icy, the teeth were welded together. Inside were the Schermer brothers' base maps that, unbelievably, I'd been told to take home the very night before the shop was closed down. I worked from them overnight; it was a special topographical job which the others on the team were to complete by the end of the next day. Now, with my own modifications, and without any fear of incurring a legal suit, I could use the maps however I wanted. Not plagiarism but a starting point. With fresh colors, clearer symbols, and a simpler lettering than I'd had to use in the past, they'd serve as the base for my new topographical series: Breslauer's World. Of course, there would also be the local needs—the statistical maps for civil and commercial interests, and a series on the city's environs, its streets and general property.

"Are you married?" she said.

"No."

"Then how many are you?" She indicated my luggage. "Are you looking for only one or will there be others coming after?"

There was a gust of wind. Even with my collar up, the cold still slipped down my neck. "No others." I stamped my numb feet. "I'm here alone. These are some of my supplies. I'm a mapmaker."

She smiled, the corners of her mouth barely curling. "Then you should be able to find your own way around the town! And to ask me for directions to those others' rooms, when we're all competing for the same tenants, well—!" With a dismissive laugh, she handed over the *Kompass*. "You might as well take this back."

Stung, I began to gather up my bags and heard: "Wait. Give me a moment to find the keys. The rooms are directly across the street. I don't share walls with my tenants."

Loaded down, I followed her across Ludwigstrasse, trying to keep my feet in the prints she made in the piles of slush. Frau Hofflinger had thrown a sweater across her shoulders and the flat red sleeves flailed between us, reaching over and over for something they had no power to grasp.

"Number forty-two," she called, pointing with a bare elbow. "The rooms are on the ground floor. The top unit is filled."

With relief, I set the bags down on the tile floor in the building's unlit common entry. Frau Hofflinger had gone ahead. She was standing at the door to the apartment but I saw her making no move to open it. She had both arms around herself.

I asked, "Are we waiting for someone to let us in?"

She reached into her pocket. Shaking out the keys as if they were wet, she selected one silvery finger from the handful, and replied scornfully, "Who? Do you think there's someone inside?"

She pushed the key into the lock. "Tell me, Herr Breslauer, do you own any property?"

"No."

"Well, I'm sure you will one day." She gave the door a sharp tug forward. "Most people want property, but why I don't know. If my husband hadn't inherited this building, I wouldn't be doing this."

The landlady stood a second at the open door, then placing her hand over her nose and mouth, she hurried inside.

I took one breath and did the same. The hallway was dim but it looked clean. A small table stood against the long wall. The hallway widened into a half-parlor, and I saw a larger table and a small green loveseat.

"Would you please go back, Herr Breslauer, and open the window in the front room? This is the first I've been in here. I received notice from my tenants not very long ago."

I pushed aside the window's lace curtain. A card fell out from behind it: *My Sweetest, happy birthday, you're 19! I love you, Torgood.* I placed it back on the sill, in a square of fresh cold air.

"Here's the culprit," she called. "In the kitchen."

I went back. She was holding a geranium. It was both limp and bloom-heavy, lying over the side of its pot. "The soil's rancid. Look! I think he poured milk on it instead of water. I'm sure he meant to save this for my next tenant, but you know what can happen when you're rushing."

I glanced about the yellow kitchen. The fire was out in the grate. The stove was cold but looked workable. A small ice-box stood in the corner, a table and two chairs, even pots and pans hanging by their handles from a metal rack. It was more than I'd expected. Happily I thought: *Good. Mine.*

Frau Hofflinger continued, "I'll have to come back to sort through things. The flat comes furnished, but some of his personal items are still here. Just look at the pantry."

"He lived here alone?"

"He had a wife. Torgood and Gerda. The Stellas. There were two of them." She went to the door to the left of the stove and deposited the dead geranium in the alley outside. "See how quickly it's done?" she said, coming back in. Her hair was netted in fresh flakes. "That's the benefit of living on the ground floor, you can easily get rid of what you don't want." She left the door open a ways to keep the air moving.

"I lived on the ground floor in Munich," I offered.

She smiled widely; it made her attractive, tilting her features into some kind of harmony. "Do you like this, then? You can have it if you do. It's really a sweet little place but anything empty will have a bad smell. I hate having it empty like this. Do you want it?"

I surveyed the kitchen one more time. "Is it quiet?"

"Oh, you won't be bothered, Herr Breslauer, I promise you! Nothing happens around here. At the most you get a yowling cat, but these days, not even that. As for the family, upstairs, I've never had a complaint about them." The land-lady picked an embroidered dishtowel from the floor and wiped her hands on it. "To be honest, the postman will be your only nuisance. He'll summon you to the door over noth-ing—over bills—when he could just as easily slip any mail through the slot. Oh, I know all about that postman. Ever since August. Ever since Herr Hofflinger was sent to Poland by his company to help the government build some new kind of factory. I shouldn't even mention it, but it's been taking forever." She threw the towel onto the table.

"Now, the bedroom is at the back. I would have had the flat cleaned, but if you want to move in tonight, you'll have to accept it as is and I'll come back when you've gone. Do you think you'll be away from home in the morning or the afternoon? I'd prefer to come after the mail arrives."

Once she let herself out, I went to the pantry and selected two of the tins of chopped ham from the shelf. I opened them then and there, and ate them standing up. Too tired to do much of anything else, I wandered once through the apartment to shut the front window and then back to the kitchen to secure that door. I washed up with cold water directly in the kitchen sink, wiping my face with the dish-towel already smudged by the landlady's fingers.

I wouldn't unpack, I decided. Instead, I went into the bedroom, pulled back the quilt, and with the flat of my hand, brushed the stray hairs off the sheet. I got in, facing the window where the snow, forced by the storm against the glass, formed white, islandlike shapes.

Above, the floorboards began creaking. Then two shoes thumped down and a piece of furniture was pushed back or pulled forward. Outside, a police siren began to whine.

One of the mapmaker's skills is walking with a measured stride to count off distance and surface. When I stepped from the apartment at dawn, the sky was almost lurid—that is, lurid with the clarity that always follows any kind of torment. Everything was still; the snow was piled pure and white above the layer of slush; the cold was crisp enough to snap. I pulled my collar up closer to my neck and set off, stopping at each corner to mark down street names, number of paces, direction, coordinates. In such a way, I would come to know my new city.

Until you look at a map—with some of the details in the area selected and retained, others just as decisively swept out of the picture—you can't quite see the place itself; you can't see how it compares to any other place. Ludwigstrasse was from end to end 322 meters long; the juncture with Osterstrasse, which ran to the north, came at 142 meters. Oster led to Gringeld, Gringeld flowed east to Tottenstrasse and dead-ended at the flag-ringed FranzJosefplatz. There a café was open and I went in to warm up and have breakfast. The waiter congenially gave me directions to the police station so I could register my new address. (East for 700 meters, he said, then: "Follow Kempener, even though Bergenstrasse is a more direct route. Cut across the commercial district; the station is in the west corner.")

But at the juncture of Kempener and Bergenstrasse, I saw a sign for a printer's shop. And I needed a printer. Why wait to find one until after I had some statistical jobs lined up? That was the usual method, sure, but with my base maps, I could start off with the topographical work, print up the first copies in the series of Breslauer's World, and draw my initial customers that way. What a turnaround, using the dream to bring in the drudge work!

I turned left, down Bergenstrasse. Within a dozen or so strides, I saw planks nailed across the windows and doors of M. Eichler's Clothiers, Weiss' Ladieswear, Our Own Restaurant, Swartz's Pharmaceuticals. Every third shop was boarded up. The yellow leaflet affixed to each closed storefront read: GOVERNMENT AUCTION: FEBRUARY 8, 1940. All along its length, though, the sidewalk was freshly shoveled, with sand scattered so that pedestrians wouldn't slip. Kreiswald's Jew street was still open for business. A tailor's shop—open, a pawnbroker's.

Premier Printers. A merry tinkling of bells announced my entrance through the front door. The air smelled lush, though by the overcoat the secretary wore I knew it was barely heated. It was the smell of ink coming off the machines in the back room, infusing everything.

"I'd like to speak with someone about a printing job. Is this firm capable of handling maps?"

"One moment, I'll get Herr Volkmann." The secretary stood up from her desk.

"Thank you, Sarah."

She stiffened, and then she nodded. Smiling slightly, she went on to the back room. With the new laws all German Jews had been given special first names. Males were assigned the name Israel, females Sarah. This was only the second occasion I'd used the address. The bookkeeper Zweigler back in Munich was the other, when I'd gone back to her for the pay due me, since I was moving on.

A man no older than I entered the front room. He was in his shirtsleeves, red-cheeked and flushed, with finely drawn—that is, almost Aryan—features. "May I help you, Herr—?"

"Breslauer."

"Herr Breslauer." His light-colored eyes flickered over my face. "I need only one moment to fix you in mind so I won't forget. Well I'm Herr Volkmann, as you must have guessed. I hear you have some maps you'd like me to see?" He held out his right hand, stained blue at the fingertips.

With a laugh, I drew the scrap of paper only partway out of my coat pocket. "This, I hope, will never be printed. It's just a newcomer's first survey of his surroundings. I haven't been here since I was a boy, but I'll be opening a shop very soon. My actual cartography is complicated, highly sophisticated, and I need to find a good printer who can handle it—at a good price."

"Ah, yes, a good price." He turned slightly. "Would you get me a pen, please, Frau Gorowitz? No, wait, the one I like is still in my jacket, I'll get it." He walked over to the wall rack and from behind the lapel of a blue suitcoat withdrew a slim ebony pen.

"As a draftsman, I'm sure you understand how important such things are," he commented, smiling. "This pen has a fine steel tip, and the shaft is well-balanced. Now, if you're talking about a four-color map, and a run of, let's say, oh, fifty or more, the numbers would start at something like this. Of course, we'd need to see the work first to come to a final agreement." He wrote a series of figures on a piece of paper.

I studied it and though the prices were low, too low in fact, I held my tongue. With a little shrug, I put the slip down on the counter.

"I see." He paused. "We both know that there are other printers, Herr Breslauer. Even as a newcomer you must have guessed that. But the reality is they're not situated here, as I am, on Bergenstrasse. And they won't be as eager to get your business—new, unestablished, with no guarantee you will have enough cash coming in to even repay—" He wet his lips. "Though anyone can see you will prove an honorable man."

"Thank you."

He tore up the piece of paper. "Let's start again. I'm sure we can come to an agreement." When he finished, he carefully put the top back on his pen.

This time the figures were even lower. "I appreciate this," I said, picking up the new slip. "I think we'll run off a smaller batch at first, rather than a larger one. Given our army's success—that is, the way borders have been falling, I don't want to do a lot of work for nothing. I'll return as soon as I'm sure I have something that will stay current for a while."

He looked up, eyes fierce. "The whole world isn't going to

change," he said. "That would be impossible."

"Well, you're probably right, but who can be sure?" I opened the door to the sound of tinkling bells. "I'm glad I met you, Israel. And I'll be back—with some luck, even before you think."

But whatever luck I had with Volkmann fled the moment I stepped inside the police station to register at my new address. I'd presented my papers and Aryan purity certificate to the clerk and had begun to swear to their authenticity when the station commander strolled over. With his thumb, he turned the citizens' registry toward him. He leaned over the counter.

"Well, how do you like this, Prudmann?" he said, and he whistled through his teeth.

The clerk said, "Commander Terskan?" He looked up with an unnerving little smile, a child's grin in an older man's face.

Midsalute, I moved away from the flag, lowered my arm. But he waved me on. "No, finish swearing."

I did so, quickly, and turned back to him.

Commander Terskan pointed at the line I'd just completed signing. "Breslauer, Felix N.?"

I nodded.

"Now of forty-two Ludwigstrasse, number one?"

"Yes."

"Recently vacant? Very recently?"

I said, "That's what I was told by the landlady. She hadn't even cleaned it up yet. I've only secured it for two weeks, as a trial. I didn't bring very much to Kreiswald with me, to set myself up, that is." I hesitated. "Is something wrong? I don't know yet which areas of town are decent and which aren't."

"Didn't you write down here that you're a mapmaker, Herr Breslauer?" said the commander.

"Yes. From Munich."

"Well, then—*Munich!*" He shrugged in a mock-helpless manner. "Kreiswald won't mystify you very much longer then. You'll soon figure it out. It usually takes a man no more than a walk to tell the good, clean neighborhoods from those that need a good cleaning. Your neighborhood," said Terskan, glancing again at the register, "is fine, but you might expect a visit in the next day or two. You might have something—oh, not that it's yours—but there could be something in your possession that its owner wants back. I'll let you know tomorrow. Would that be all right?" He smiled, his white teeth straight, square.

"Of course."

"Prudmann, see that Herr Breslauer isn't delayed any longer. Herr Breslauer," he said, with a nod.

Prudmann pulled the register over the counter, made a mark by what must have been my name. Then, humming a little nursery song, he got out a duplicate book, but with a red cover, and opened it to a blank page. He began to record my information.

"Is there something—?" I ventured.

"No," mumbled the clerk. "Don't bother yourself." He bent his head and continued writing. "You're done here."

With a shaking hand I closed the station's heavy door behind me. The wind had picked up and with it the snow. For a second, I stood confused by the swirls of traffic on the other side of the curb, then I headed for Kempener. Kempener to FranzJosefplatz, to—? I wouldn't take Bergenstrasse, even though it was the more direct route.

I knew what Terskan had been saying. I'd acted too quickly. Too readily, I'd assumed that Isaac and Stefan Schermer had gone. But maybe they hadn't. Maybe it had been just as the bookkeeper had said, just some emergency. And with it resolved, their arms and legs swinging, those large heads held high, they'd returned to their building; with glee they ripped down that sign and inside again they saw who—and what—was missing.

A set of base maps: missing. Felix Breslauer: missing.

I hurried, head down against the wind, not counting my strides. I'd been reported for stealing property. Before me, the pavement kept disappearing, trackless and white.

The door to my apartment was partway open. I heard someone rummaging around, pausing, then rummaging around again, quickly, as if searching against time for some treasure. Shaking, I kicked off my snow-clotted boots in the common entry and just left them; my socks were damp. "Is that you, Frau Hofflinger?" I called.

"Come in, Herr Breslauer. I'm in the parlor."

I had to stop myself from running forward. She was the only person I knew in Kreiswald.

"The mail was early." She turned around in front of the bureau; her hands were clasped before her stomach. Again, she wore the red sweater but this time she wore it fully, tightly, over a brown dress—the sleeves rounded, the buttons closed except for the highest one, at the neck. "It didn't matter." She gave that odd, slanted smile. "Herr Hofflinger is no writer."

Steadying my voice, I said, "It's not a good time."

She wasn't sure what I was talking about, I could tell. She turned her face to the side, with her chin lifted just a bit, as if that would help her to make clearer sense of what I'd really meant. She looked as if she would concentrate very hard on what I'd say next.

I stuck my hands in the pockets of my coat. "You have to leave. I have to work and can't have you here."

"Oh! I thought we'd agreed that if you were out—" she hesitated. "But you're back now. Yes, of course, I'll leave you to your work." Coloring slightly, she took a breath. Her chin lifted and with the clear tone of a much younger woman she said: "I'll come back once more. And I can tell you that I can't just go back and forth at your whim. I have other obligations. This is at your choice."

She picked up a wastebasket filled with paper—envelopes and letters and such. "Old correspondence, I suppose." The landlady laughed in such a way that I knew she had read some of them. "I've got some other things packed up in the kitchen. I'll take that bag out, too."

She walked back, her shoes clicking so loudly, each heel-strike so distinctly separate one from the other, it seemed the apartment I'd rented was empty, that there was nothing in it—no furniture, no curtains or rugs—nothing to absorb the shock of anyone's walking through it.

I went after her.

"Are you following me?" She turned around from the kitchen table in much the same way she had before the parlor bureau, with her hands clasped over her stomach. Calmly she said, "I'm not taking it all. I left you half the food in the pantry and a quarter of the coal in the back bin. Imagine leaving coal when there's a shortage! He could have sold it, if only back to the delivery man." She rubbed her eyes. "I'll have to return for it, but you can see how much there is. Of course I can't just carry it off in my arms."

"Bring a wheelbarrow."

She laughed. "I haven't had time to go through the rest of the apartment. When do you want me to return?"

"Tomorrow—late in the afternoon." The words stuck like ice on my tongue. "Come then. You can have a free hand. Take whatever you want of theirs. It's not mine, I wouldn't touch it."

* * *

A few moments later, alone in the bright, strange apartment, I slid the base maps from my portfolio and onto the
kitchen table. The full series of the earth's surface fanned out
before me. Among them *Northern Europe #3, highlights:
Finland, Sweden, Norway, and Denmark.* I separated it
from the others. Then, sitting with my back to the stove, I
placed a sheet of tracing paper—that reptile's eyelid—atop
it and began the work that would not only save me but also,
when I was safe, give me something to use.

First: Norway, wedged high against the top frame. I
brought it down just a notch. My pencil veered just slightly
away from the Schermers' shadow-country lying two paper
strata beneath it. I pressed harder and the new border thickened. Finland (already gone) had to be drawn with a lighter
hand, and where the base map maintained the boundary,
the new one claimed instead the merger; where the shadow
said: chasm, the new corrected it: no, hardly a crack. I went
next to Denmark. Then to Sweden, a dangling arm; it had
to reach—but downward to Rostock, also ours, *already* ours.
I looked again at Rostock, its position against the coordinates.

When the map was traced, but not as some lackey would
trace it, I stood up and went over to the stove. In my hands
was the Schermers' original. It seemed to head toward the
coals on its own. For one breath it lay lightly atop them, then
it just lifted and its edges crumpled together. Petaled like
that, like an impossibly bright rose, it burned. The brief
conflagration added no heat to the room that I could notice.

The work went slowly. By five in the morning, I had traced
the outlines and the most common features of only a half-
dozen of the European maps. So many others remained. And
I was trying only for base maps, only for something simple
to build from! I had the three full maps I'd completed back

in Munich, but so what? I'd have to destroy what I couldn't copy. That would give me not even one-fifth of the series. It was no use.

I wandered into the front room. Piled under the frosted window was my luggage. Seeing everything I owned still packed away just sparked something in me. Damn these things! I'd leave them all, start again somewhere else, in some different way. Perhaps only a clerk?

This could be the last chance. I seized my overcoat. With only the small duffle in hand for my shaving kit and such, I let myself out of the apartment. In the pre-dawn air, Ludwigstrasse was frozen into position. I shivered. For a moment I stood on the stoop, stamping my boots and looking up at a lamp glowing in Frau Hofflinger's upstairs corner window. Then I was halfway down the street and heading toward the train station.

Yet as I approached the depot from behind the news kiosk, the one in the middle of the intersection, I saw two lines of soldiers flanking the front entrance. They stood with rifles at the ready; at different intervals, a small explosion of breath puffed up before each of their faces.

I glanced at the array of magazines and papers on the kiosk counter. The vendor didn't notice me; he was pinning the front page of the paper to the back wall.

"Hurry up!" someone ordered. Almost immediately, fifty or sixty people surged around the corner of Frankenstrasse. A strange, ill-matched group. Bundled up against the cold, their faces looked swollen and flushed as one's face is when just lifted from a pillow after a short night's rest. Stateless, probably. Jews. Old people and younger, and very young—children, all rounding the corner and spreading into the street without talking.

"Hurry, I told you!" It was an officer who said it, now I saw him, at the back of the group. At the sound of his voice, the soldiers raised their rifles and the people at the front of the crowd hesitated. The captain repeated his command, but this time in Slovak. As he said it, he crouched and with both gloves scooping, flung the sopping handfuls of slush at them. "Go," he shouted in German, throwing again. "Get out of here, filth. Go back where you came from!" The balls splattered against their hats and necks and set off a flurry of small, startled cries. Awkwardly, they pressed forward, filing between the guards, the adults holding the children's hands, the very oldest ones holding each other. Everyone held some kind of bag no larger than mine. As the captain went through, smacking his wet gloves together, the soldiers formed a wedge before the entrance, blocking it off. Standing to the side were two police officers; I hadn't noticed them. The patrolmen were talking to each other; their breath floated like café smoke about their heads.

As casually as I could, I turned back to the counter. I put the duffle down on a bank of snow and picked up the *Kompass*. The headline concerned Russia's breaking off relations with Norway.

The vendor was still tidying up his wares.

"I want this paper," I said.

"Didn't see you." He came forward. "Sorry to hold you up."

I dropped the coins in his gloved palm. Casually again, I picked up the duffle, and with no other option, I turned back, in the direction I'd just come from.

I was almost to my building when I heard someone chasing after me on the crunching snow. "Herr Breslauer," called the landlady. "Stop."

I turned. As if in triumph, she waved an envelope over her head. It looked as if she'd just come from bed. Clad in a thin white housecoat, with her hair loose and wild over her shoulders, she stretched one leg out and then—tightrope walker—the other, along the icy pavement.

"So," I shouted back, despite myself, "you finally have gotten your letter—from Poland, that is."

After a taxi went by, she crossed the street and came up to me. "Not at all," she said with a little grimace, one hand against her bare throat. "You have."

I took the envelope. The flap was sealed with the black wax imprint of the Kreiswald Police. "Frau Hofflinger." With a click of my heels, I pocketed it and turned away.

She followed, talking. "A policeman delivered it. An older man who looked very uncomfortable. I suppose he didn't want to leave it under your door. They usually don't, with official business." She paused. "They had my name from the citizens' registry. As your landlady, they must think I have some responsibility."

I didn't answer. I opened the door to the building.

"It's so early to be out, Herr Breslauer." She looked at the duffle bag as I fiddled with the keys.

"I worked through the night. It's no use bothering to get any sleep after that. You can't make it up." The door swung open and I went in without taking off my boots.

She slipped in, too, saying, "You're right. I'll make you some hot coffee. I know the kitchen and you look exhausted." The sharp sweetness of almond extract floated from her in a kind of homey perfume.

"Frau Hofflinger—"

"No, attend to your business, I won't bother you." She waved a pale arm over her shoulder. Her shoes left small wet tracks on the floor.

I waited until she was well back in the apartment, and then I took out the envelope. Just as I slid my thumbnail under the sealing wax, I remembered the Schermers' base maps. In my haste, I'd left them lying on the kitchen table.

My mouth went dry. I had hung myself.

"Frau Hofflinger!" I called, running.

She looked up, those blue eyes wide and at the same time narrowed. She was holding *Central Europe #4* before her as if it were a hymnal. "All the details," she said. "How do you know all these things?"

"Put it down."

She let it slide from her hands, on top of the others. "I didn't bend it."

"Bending doesn't matter. Just the oil in your fingers can leave marks on it. That's my work, my livelihood." I went over and began to gather my maps, corner by corner.

"It's so nice and warm in here," she said, trying for conversation. "Maybe it feels even warmer when the coal comes free." Her voice trailed off. Upstairs, someone began to walk around in the kitchen.

I looked at her. "The kettle is over on the stove, Frau Hofflinger." Surreptitiously I slipped the remaining Schermer maps under the bottom of the pile.

"Oh yes," she said, relieved, "I see it."

Back in the parlor, I separated out the two groups of maps and, getting down on my knees, slid the originals beneath the bureau. I put the copies into the leather portfolio where the others had been.

Then I unfolded the letter, the crisp, white paper. *17 January 1940. Herr Felix Breslauer: Anything left behind in your new home should be thrown out. Heil Hitler. R. Terskan, Commander.*

I sat down on the floor, stunned. Was I safe? I read the letter again and broke into laughter. "You pig!" With a whoop, I pried off my boots and threw them together across the room into the stack of luggage. The pile wavered, toppled. I raised my hands up over my head, victorious.

"What was that," she called.

"The gods on high," I shouted, "bowling!"

I went into the kitchen. I pulled out the chair in which I'd worked all night and sat down, tilting it back on its rear legs. "Tell me," I said, "is it usual for your police to meddle in people's business this way?" And I handed her the note.

She read it, her lips pursed. "No," she muttered.

"Well, I didn't think so."

Letting out a breath, she said, "Gerda Stella moved out of this apartment to be with Rolf Terskan. She left so quickly, she didn't take anything with her. No one talks about it, but it's true. I suppose he wanted to be considerate to her about her old attachments. That's what this must be."

The chair came down. "It wasn't the war? But from how you kept speaking of his, that Torgood's, distress I thought—"

"Not war. Adultery." Frau Hofflinger cut me off with a slashing motion of her left hand. "The marriage fell apart. They were sweet together, I can tell you that, and young. But on the other hand, Commander Terskan—he was Torgood's commander, you know. Well, that part is over with, too. Torgood was transferred to Passau. Passau's far, but not as far as Poland. Do you take sugar?" She set the bowl on the table. "He left some."

I looked up. "Why do you say that only he left it? She did, too."

"You're right, I suppose." Frau Hofflinger used the embroidered towel to pick up the hot kettle. "After everything's said and done, what *has* been done doesn't matter. The sugar's here, that's all." She bent her wrist and from out of the kettle came a thin, hot stream of coffee. Even though it was ersatz, it was richly dark.

I picked up my cup and took a huge gulp. It tasted wonderful, nearly scorching my throat. "So, Gerda took nothing from here?" I said.

She tilted her head. "Didn't you look in the closets?"

"I was focused on my work. You know what a bachelor is like, working faithfully all through the night. But if there is something you saw that you want—"

"I saw—" her voice trembled, and she stopped.

"Without empty space, I can't unpack." I drained my cup.

Frau Hofflinger bit her lower lip and put down the kettle. Without another word she went to the bedroom. I heard her open the closet.

"She doesn't need a scrap like this any longer," she called. "You should see how fancy she is these days."

"Let me see." I picked up her cup and took a sip.

She came back into the kitchen. Over the white bathrobe she had draped a fox stole. The legs hung down, the tiny, flattened paws just grazing her breasts and against her bare collarbone rested the head with its stitched-shut eyes and thin snout. The jaws were only slightly opened. Frau Hofflinger herself was flushed. Perhaps nervously, she kept stroking the fox along its full length, where the spine would have been. "Do you mean I should take this?"

Carefully I resettled her cup in the saucer. "Either that or throw it out."

"How simple!"

I looked up and she laughed, pale throat glistening.

"But you look lovely," I said, startled. "That is, in this fur, in this light, with your hair, and your face—already shaped so like a heart—"

Her smile faded. "You think that?" she said, and tucked the black tip of the fox's tail into its mouth as I stood up.

She was on her side, away from me when I rolled from the sheets. I got dressed as quickly and quietly as I could; I didn't want to wake her. There was so much more I could still make of this day. It was a wonderful day! I gathered up the few things I needed and as I shut the door first to my apartment, then the heavier one to Frau Hofflinger's—dear Erika's—building, I felt buoyant, a different man entirely from just half a day before. Briskly I walked down Ludwigstrasse, turned right and right again.

In no time at all my hand was on the doorknob of Premier Printers. I entered and Sarah looked up.

"I'll get Herr Volkmann," she said, pushing away from her desk.

"Do that, please."

He came in from the back room. His face was bright and shiny with perspiration. "I'm glad to see you this soon, Herr Breslauer," he said, coming up to the counter.

"I've been able to get a lot done. Two maps for certain; one other, possibly. But I'll wait on that last just a bit."

"Well, fine." He paused. "May I see?"

I laid the portfolio down on the counter.

He turned the case toward him and began to unzip it. As he did, I said, "I noticed some of the property on this street is going to be auctioned. That gives me something to think about."

He looked up sharply. "Oh?"

"Sure. Maybe I will be your neighbor." I reached over to flip open the cover. Then the maps were spilling out.

"What good is a boy," said the Inspector of National Political Educational Institutions, SS Senior Group Leader Heissmeyer, "who is endowed with great intellectual gifts but who for the rest is a weak, hopelessly irresolute, and slack fellow? We have in mind the ideal of the lively youngster who comes from good parents with hereditary virtues, who is physically sound, full of courage, and brings with him spiritual exuberance and alertness."

—the *Hamburger Fremdenblatt*
December 30, 1941

The Tryout

As LONG AS he was invisible, Franzel and I played each day after school. Freed from obedience in the girls' classroom, I'd race home, heels kicking the air of Heinzstrasse, Ringstrasse and Königstrasse, before stopping at my door: Osterwaldplatz 23. With a shout to Mother: "I'm changing out of my school uniform!" I'd dump my books down on my chair— "Peti's place," I called it.

In our family, each child could claim complete sovereignty over a single piece of furniture. Mine was the walnut chair that had been Mother's great-aunt's. Janna Ruthe Benteimer had died before photography was much used to record common people's features, but I was sure I knew just how she looked because of the chair. She too had slender arms and legs, with tight fists, pointed toes, and a somewhat too large head and seat. Though a bit darker than the usual fashion, her finish was still so pleasing and smooth that she could fit into the most uniform of groupings. Mother's stories about Great-Aunt Benteimer—"What a charmer, what a member of the optimist society! Wherever she went, she'd find herself among friends. Where did they all come from?"—only confirmed that at age six, when my time came to learn about the rights and responsibilities which went along with possession, I'd made the right choice. Resting my hand on the cool brown, tightly furled fist, I stated: "I like this one."

My brothers had claimed their own furniture years before my chance had arrived. In fact, Wilhelm and Thomas were out of the home—gone to military school and the army—by the time I was six. About them I knew most intimately the gold-braided horsehair hassock (Wilhelm) and the hickory writing table with its secret back drawer and false front (Thomas). Between Thomas and me had come three other children. Their little profiles, cut from black silhouette paper and mounted in three black, mourning-draped frames, hung in the hall at the top of the stairs. The memorial inscriptions read only: "Hendrik—one and one half months. 1924." "Angelica—eleven days. 1926." "Hendrika Angelica—one year, eight and one-half months. 1930." The silhouettes were claimed by my parents, though they never said so aloud. But I saw how they always touched the wall as they walked past it, as if downstairs and in secret, they'd first touched their fingers to their lips and only in this sly, hidden way could they finally release the kisses.

"Peti?" Mother called, "are you back? Come show yourself to me; I'm outside. Erna's here."

Erna was the washerwoman who took away our heavy, soiled bedding and towels every second Wednesday and returned them cleaned on Friday. For the lighter wash she used the tubs we kept at our house. I pushed open the back door from the kitchen. Between the fruit trees the lines sagged under the weight of wet clothes. Mother and Erna were almost entirely hidden by the dank shapes, but I could see the hems of two identically flowered aprons and, beneath those, two pairs of legs. The thinner, pale legs were

Mother's; a few strands of her reddish hair were caught up in the breeze and floated above the line. "Come here," she called again.

"But Franzel's waiting for me in the secret place."

"Petra! None of your stories, please. I'm late for the Women's Alliance and Erna can't do this by herself. Get over here."

I nodded, and ducked between Mother's yellow nightgown and dressing robe. The touch of wet cotton made me shiver. It was October, and although the sun was out, the air could be chilly.

"Hello, Fräulein Peti," said Erna, bending down to pluck from the sodden tangle of trousers and sleeves in the wicker basket, my other school uniform. As she handed it over, the brown skirt unfolded as slowly as an accordion. "This can go on the short line without dragging on the ground. If you would do it for me, that would be a great help."

"The clothespins are over there." Mother indicated the blue cloth bag with a jut of her chin, since both of her hands were busily trying to fasten the shoulders of Papa's wet dressing robe, next to her own. "I can't work much longer," she muttered. "This is too important a meeting for me to miss."

I took my handful of wooden pegs around the tree to where the short childish line began its empty grin.

"Then you must go, of course," said Erna. "Fräulein Peti and I will finish up with no problem."

But Mother snorted in disgust. "I'm not looking forward to this, Erna. Really, it's not as if the Women's Alliance made up the new laws."

"Of course not, Frau Worshafter. Who would say that?"

"Surely the Jews understand the predicament, surely, after all the projects we've worked on together, they know us. If there were to be bad blood between us now, because of this—"

I fit the waistband of my skirt right up to the taut rope, trying not to double it over, so it would dry out evenly.

"Oh, they'll go," Erna said amiably. "No one wants to be where they're not wanted."

"I just can't do it," burst out Mother, shaking Father's robe. "Look at Herr Worshafter's robe. I *knew* you should have taken it with the bedding. It belongs with the heavier articles, not out here, where the line is so flimsy."

"Please," said the washerwoman, "move over a little, if you would, Frau Worshafter, and hand me the pins. I can fasten it in place."

By now, Franzel was already in our secret spot. A tingle went up my spine: it was his turn to hide. If I were in the field behind Ilse Kohler's house, where I had hoped to be, I'd have my head in my arms, my arms against the fence, my eyes staring at my shoes, and I'd be counting at the top of my voice: One-fifteen, two-sixteen, three-seventeen. . . . Only at the combination of ten-twenty-four could I look up.

Where was my friend?

Turning, tiptoe silent, I'd watch as a hunter does, for even one flicker of the tall grasses. "You're caught," I'd cry, gleeful, lying. "I see you!" I'd wait as the boast skimmed and faded.

The field stretched out. Low purple with clover and dotted abundantly with meadow flowers, it was nothing like the waxy drawings I made of it in school. That a nine-year-old could hide himself between its delicate grassy lines and completely disappear seemed astounding. Among the crowds of shoppers and stacks of wooden crates in the Grubenplatz vegetable market, anyone could get lost. Or in the spruce grove that began at the middle bridge over the river. Full of shadows and secret twistings, the grove stitched its dark needles all the way east, past the border. *That* was a good place to go if you wanted not to be seen. But in a field so flat and clear that the sky met the land as a window meets its own sill?

Once, I asked him how could someone be out in the open and yet clean out of view?

"It's because," Franzel whispered, sneaking behind me so his words puffed into my ear, "I like being invisible. And I know something more."

I didn't turn, didn't even try to tag him. "What?"

"You like searching for me."

"How do you know that?"

The grass ruffled, making barely a whisper. "Because I know you."

At that, such a warmth spread across my belly, I had to wrap my arms about my stomach and give a little squeeze. When Ilse Kohler looked out her window, there I was, hugging myself, kneeling in the weeds.

"Get out of here, Peti," she shouted. "I didn't say you could be here. It's my father's land, not yours, I told you that before. Hurry up or I'll tell my brother and he'll make you go."

I twisted around. "We're leaving," I called, quickly.

"What? Are you with that boy, too? Where is he? I warned you, Peti!"

"I've got to tie my shoes, sorry!" I crouched down in the white-petaled asters, where Franzel was, and swatted aside the gangly, ticklish stems. He was grinning. Something black, a poppyseed, maybe, was wedged into the gap between his front teeth.

"She didn't see you," I exulted. "I can't believe it."

He shrugged and his thin shoulders went almost to his ears. "I told you," he whispered, "I like being invisible. If she hadn't caught you, we could play all day."

"Stay still." I wet the tip of two fingers on my tongue, then reached through the stems and, in the same way Mother and Papa seemed barely to brush the upstairs wall, I daubed up the black speck. It had wings; they were nearly transparent, outlined a pale yellow. "See this?" I breathed. "A gnat. I saved you. You nearly swallowed it."

"When are you leaving, Peti?" shouted Ilse. "I'm waiting."

I flicked the ruined insect toward a patch of rye grass. "Just a moment! I had to bury something. All right—going!"

"You—what?"

Stifling our laughter, Franzel and I raced bent double in opposite directions. I looked back once; there: the top of his head, that dark dot darting suddenly here and there above the rye.

When I reached the dirt road, I turned around, standing to my full height. "Until tomorrow, Franzel!"

"Petra," said Mother sharply. She stood in front of the line on which Father's robe was splayed open. It had been pinned at the edges as if it were a whole, curving chicken breast fixed for lying flat in the broiler. "I want you to do whatever Erna tells you."

Said Erna, "Now don't trouble yourself, Frau Worshafter. We'll do the job ahead of us, as we all must, of course, without fuss."

Mother reached into her apron pocket. "Thank you," she said, pressing some reichsmarks into the washerwoman's plump hand.

"Are you going, Mama?"

She untied the apron and lifted it over her head before answering she wasn't sure how late she might be. "I don't want you returning alone to an empty house. I don't like the idea of that! You can't go out to play, Peti. Stay inside and go over your tables, as the teacher told you to do—until your father comes home."

I bit my lip. Papa never returned before six, and then we would have to eat supper, and then after that it would be night. Franzel's parents were even more strict than mine. At one minute after sunset, he had to be home, the door locked behind him. "What are your parents afraid of?" I'd once asked when we saw the sun slipping from the top bar of Herr Simon's west fence. "What are yours?" he'd countered. Then he picked up a stone and disappeared through the reddening blades of the field.

Mother tied her flowered apron, dampened in spots, around me. "You'll stay right here and help Erna work, won't you?"

The washerwoman's broad pale face and blue eyes appeared above the line. "Come and join me. It makes the time go faster when there are two."

I picked up the clothespin bag and brought it over.

"You're a good girl, Fräulein Peti," she said, squeezing out two of Papa's black socks. "Are you in tomorrow's gymnastics showcase?"

"I might go to watch."

"Oh, you should go. My Fritz will be performing on the rings. Do you know what they are? They hang from ropes and you have to balance between them."

Five years older than I, silvery-haired Fritz was a squat, wide-boned boy, all shoulders and hands. I could well imagine him grabbing on to the iron circles and slowly swiveling up from the floor, like a metal screw that had no wood to burrow into but was determined nevertheless to spin about in the air.

"You must go," urged Erna, "everyone has been practicing so hard. Maybe by the next showcase, in March, you'll be a member too. By then you won't be so young. Fritz told me that all the children who are fit are expected to join once they turn eight. It's more than the exercise, it's about being part of a group, Fräulein Peti. Aren't you in the German Girls' League?"

I made a face. "In school. Everyone is."

"Do you like it?"

I shook my head.

"But you must," she chided. "Don't you like to get badges?"

I bit my lip. All we did was the same thing, again and again, sit and listen to the Führer's teachings and then practice marching on the flat field behind the school. We drilled so we could march behind the band without looking wrong. You looked wrong when you didn't keep your shoulders back or when your chin wasn't level. Looking wrong, said Frau Hessler, the girls' leader, showed disloyalty to the Führer. Her own head erect, she'd have us march in place. One! Two. She shouted at the top of her voice. One! Two. One! Two. One! Two.

"One day you'll get a badge," said Erna consolingly. She snapped her wrists and the socks sank exactly midshin over the rope. "Get that sweet little blouse of yours out of the basket, and I'll pin it up. I can fit it in right here, next to your mother's. There's enough room on this line."

Mother handed me a steaming bowl of broth. "Papa's," she whispered, turning back to the stove.

Carefully, I walked to the table and put it at his place. Then I pulled back his empty chair and it bumped across the rug.

Papa turned from the radio in the parlor, his hand still on the black knob. "Frieda?" he called, nodding at me, but directing his voice into the kitchen, over the urgent metallic voice of the newscaster. "Is it ready?"

Mother followed with both of our soupbowls. "Yes, come to the table," she spoke in a kind of relief.

The newscaster was saying: *Last Thursday when Great Britain rejected our offer of peace, it unwisely challenged—*

There was a click. In the silence left by the newscaster, my father stood up, a man in his middle years who liked to shove out his chest and walk with a good, firm stride.

"Tell me," he said, shaking out his napkin and turning to my mother, "how did the Alliance meeting go?"

She glanced over at me. "You may start, Peti. But slowly." She dipped her spoon in the yellow broth and stirred the liquid to cool it off a little. "It was difficult," she said, raising the filled spoon.

"Some bargaining back and forth, I take it? Accusations, too?" Papa pulled back his shoulders and wrinkled his nose. In a higher voice, clearly mimicking someone else, he waggled, " 'How can you do this to us? Yes, we're Jews, but we're part of the membership. Friends, instead of this peaceful solution, we should disband the whole organization. Instead of our having to go, let the Alliance' "—he shrugged and the air shockingly went right out of him—" 'go. Just let it fall.' "

"Yes!" Mother leaned forward. "That's just what they said—exactly. It was terrible."

"But you got through it," replied Papa in his normal voice. "And now the Alliance will pull together even more. I know how it is."

She reached over and put two fingers on his wrist. "I know you do, Stefan."

"I let two of our staff go the other week. No, no, don't sort through any pictures in your head! They were probably in the office whenever you came by, but you wouldn't have noticed them. Really, they didn't stand out."

I looked up. "They didn't?"

He shook his head. "No. Pepper, please, Frieda."

She passed him the mill. He turned the handle vigorously and the black flakes dotted his soup. Specks, little bits of

circles you could barely see, except when they fell in a swirl
against one another or over something else. There must have
been hundreds floating in his yellow dish, and a column still
falling. Then Papa's hands swung and the long mill tilted
above my bowl.

Mother said, "Did you hear what Papa just asked you,
Petra?"

I gave a start. "Excuse me?"

"Half the time she's off in some world of her own." Mother
put down her spoon. "I don't want her to isolate herself like
that. Tomorrow there's a gymnastics show, all the children
on teams. I'll see if she can join one of them; I think it's
important. Even our washerwoman was talking about it, Stefan, about how it's drawn that boy of hers out of himself."

Outside it was dreary, but the light inside the town's ath-
letic building was bright and square and the air smelled of
warm flesh and sweat and excitement. "Don't slip," an old
lady warned. She told us to wipe our shoes on the straw mats
in the entrance, then directed us to the racks to hang up our
umbrellas and damp coats.

Pulling off her scarf, Mother smoothed her hair back into
its bun. "Well, I'm glad we're finally here. Is your husband
at the rehearsal, Frau Frasier?"

To my surprise, this Frau Frasier took a blunt step backward and began to play an invisible drum. "Rat-a-tat-tat.
Rat-a-tat-tat," she said through heavily lipsticked lips.

Mother began to grin.

Continued the old lady throatily, "Helmut wouldn't miss
making so much fine noise. Herr Worshafter, I suppose, is
still a volunteer in our Citizens' Band?"

Mother swung her arms upward with a leader's emphatic
whoosh. "Yes," she said; then as suddenly: "Oh, oh no!" and
she wrenched her head about as if horrified to see a baton

flying out of her grip. The two women laughed.

"Go on in." Frau Frasier gave me a little push. "You don't want to miss anything. And look for my granddaughter, Sophi; she's in both the floor exercises and the parallel bars. Keep an eye out for the blue uniforms, the blue team. You can tell her from the others because at home I wound a nice blue ribbon through the length of her braid."

Mother took my hand. "Stay close," she instructed, leading me into the gymnasium proper just as a great cry went up. The walls were made of people, it seemed, the lines of them all crouching, roaring, shouting. Even the floor began to shake.

I pulled back. "Mama, I don't want to."

"Oh, Peti," she said, "there's no reason to be afraid. They're just excited. I promise this will turn out to be fun." She looked up into one of the stands. "Hold on to my hand, we're going to climb."

The stairs were single wood boards that gave a little with our weight; there were no backs to them, and the aisle was narrow, cluttered in the wrong places with folded coats or satchels. I had to go slowly. Mother pulled me along and I heard her calling out greetings to Doctor Rosmus, and to weasely Frau Hofflinger, who lived directly behind us, and, just after I stepped over someone's lunch box, to her friend Frau Gottschild. The higher we climbed, the quieter the crowd seemed to become. I glanced ahead and just a bit to the side: the people up here were sitting perfectly still, watching something down below us, something we'd left.

"Can we stop now?"

"No." Mother took a firmer grip of my hand, "We have to go where it's empty. Not much further. Just watch your feet."

Again, we weaved our way upwards. Far below, between the backless steps, the floor had the cool, shadowy sheen of an ice pond. How I wanted to be down there, under the stands, hidden from view! "Franzel," I whispered, "if you're down there, please look up and I'll sneak away."

Mother stopped, her face pink with exertion. "Excuse me, Commander Terskan," she said.

The police officer, who had been peering at someone at the other end of the row, now turned to us. "My pleasure," he said. He stood slowly, as if he were being poured upward from his knees. Everything about him, his broad dark face, the brown uniform, even the width of his shoulders, looked too solid in the bright artificial light of the gym. "If you please—" He stepped back and, as if he were escorting us into his car, he guided Mother in first by lightly touching her elbow, and then bent to me and cupped a large hand against the back of my neck. "There," he said and sat back down. "Enjoy the showcase."

"Would you please move over just a bit further," asked Mother, "so my little girl won't be blocked by the gentleman in front of her? I want her to be able to see everything."

Under the mustache, his mouth twitched. But he bent down and brought up from beneath his seat a damp brown greatcoat, which he refolded and placed somewhat further along under the bench. Then he slid over. "I hope she has enough room now?"

Mother thanked him again, and he settled back in against the crowd.

"Sit down, Peti. And smooth out your skirt."

I looked down to the gymnasium floor. They were between events and everything seemed disorganized. Then I saw the group of older girls in identical blue bloomers, with their arms and legs gleaming and smooth, tugging three large grey canvas pads to the center of the room. They fit the pads together and moved away, their arms straight out at their sides, to keep the space clear. All the girls with braids had blue ribbons wound through them.

The crowd rustled as five blue team girls stepped out from the milling officials and team members and went directly to the middle of the mats. They got down on their hands and knees. From different parts of the crowd came four other girls. They placed themselves—hands and knees—on top of the first five.

"Does that hurt, Mama?"

She shook her head.

"Why not?"

"It just doesn't."

Three new members of the blue team walked onto the mats. By stepping on this leg and that back, they mounted and balanced on top of the row of four; all seven—each one—became as sturdy and unwavering as a piece of furniture. Two more girls pulled themselves onto the highest three. As soon as they did, they too merged into the structure.

"Watch that one over there. Now, you'll see something," I heard Mother say, and she seized my hand as she had when we were climbing.

Standing alone at the edge of the mat, her knees bent, arms thrust forward, was the last of the blue girls. The spectators, all of us, leaned forward. With no one to block our vision of her, she seemed almost painfully exposed. She rocked back on her heels. Small, tense, her face turned away from us and toward the huge braced breathing structure, she started to run. Her heels were kicking. She made a wide-armed, scrambling leap for the top. Mother squeezed my hand. "Peti!" Mother breathed, pulling me up with her. The audience burst into applause.

In the middle of the floor, the other competitors relegated off to the sides, there, unshakable, stood a pyramid.

* * *

"And I saw a white team that worked on the balance beams, and a red team that had just competed against Landau on the parallel bars, oh—and on a horse, but it's not a horse at all, not a real one. You know what I mean, they just like to pretend it's real."

"Stop! Stop!" Franzel put his hands over his ears. "I don't care. I don't want to hear anymore about those stupid teams."

"Not so loud," I warned. I stood up and looked at Ilse's house; the windows, even through the drizzle, were dark. For four days the weather had been miserable—the clean laundry Erna had hung up was only getting wetter and wetter, and the lines were straining, nearly to the ground; but I couldn't wait any longer: I needed to come out here with Franzel. That morning, as everyone stood lined up in the schoolyard before entering the classrooms, I'd used the secret code of twisting my head around to the right twice and then to the left. This meant that we had to meet. "Listen to me," I said, squatting down in the little clearing we'd made by trampling the dripping grasses. "The showcase wasn't anything terrible, like we thought. It wasn't boring. It was fun."

He looked at me glumly. The moisture in the air turned everything the same shade of grey; the outline of his face seemed no different from the sky, the soggy weeds; even his cap, which I knew to be blue, flopped heavily over his head like a last sad grey petal. "You're going to play with them, aren't you," he said finally. "Sorry, I mean, you're going to compete with them. That's different."

"But you can, too!" My voice broke out of a whisper. "Will you?"

He shrugged.

"Tomorrow there's a medical examination. We have to be

healthy enough to join. They don't want anyone to get hurt. Come with me tomorrow, Franzel. It's the tryout."

He just sat the same way, hunched over. The drizzle turned into rain. I stood up again and peered at Ilse's house. In one of the windows, a lamp was now lit. Its yellow glow was cut by the raindrops, which, with a slight drumming, sank into the dark ground.

"Peti, I like our secret game," he insisted. "I don't want to have to play with anyone else."

"But my mother's signed me up." I crouched next to him. "Starting next Monday I'll be at practice. And no matter which team I get on, everyone goes to the athletics building and practices every day after school. I won't have any time left after that. Don't you see"—I wiped the drops off my face, the rain was coming down harder now—"that's why you have to come with me to the tryout, you *have* to come, Franzel."

Slowly he said, "All right, Peti."

The line started inside the gymnasium and backed into the front hall. Seated at the wooden table where Frau Frasier had been posted on Saturday was one of the school's senior boys; he wrote down each of our names with a thick blue pencil and then told us to hang up our coats and take off our shoes. "We don't want the floor to get wet," he pointed out, "it's very bad for the wood."

Shoes, damp at the toes, lined the tiled hall past the coat rack. All the heels were pressed against the wall as though the owners were still in them—as though the owners were stretching up from them so as to surpass last year's mark on the doctor's measuring tape.

Quickly I slipped off my pair and ran in my thin cotton socks back to the entryway for a place in line. "Hurry, Franzel," I mouthed over my shoulder. He was sitting cross-legged just behind the coat rack, still untying his wet laces. But he must have seen me because between the overcoats waved a pale hand.

I lined up behind a tall boy from grade eight. A moment later, a finger jabbed my back. But when I turned around, it wasn't Franzel.

"Hello, Peti," said Ilse Kohler, with a wide grin. "Alone? What are you doing here with all of us? Are you signing up today, too?"

No, I muttered, I'd already signed up on Saturday.

She pulled Traute Gottschild over next to her and whispered something in her ear. Traute raised her eyebrows and giggled. "We want to get on the red team," Ilse said aloud.

The line moved forward by three or four people and I slid ahead, right to the empty threshold of the double doorway.

Ilse asked, tapping my shoulder, "Which team are you trying for?"

I saw the top of Franzel's dark head just behind Traute's blond one. I shrugged. "The blue, probably." That's what Franzel and I had decided upon.

"Oh, try for red, they're much, much better. I saw them in the showcase." She leaned over and whispered in my ear, "Tell them you want to be on it with us."

Flustered, I pulled away.

She nodded vigorously. "So, will you do it?" she asked, plucking at my sleeve.

"Where are the next applicants?" a voice called out. "Little girl in the doorway, you're first, pay attention!"

I hurried forward between the empty bleachers. Only a few of the overhead bulbs were on, filling the giant room with a dark and watery light like that in an aquarium. In the dimmest section children were doing jumping exercises; others rolled around on the big canvas mats; I saw how some boys and girls filed along on a balance beam with their arms held straight out at their sides.

"Right here!" The coach smacked his clipboard down on the desk and the air seemed to leap back from his wiry body.

I stopped on the black stripe, a meter away from him. Behind me, the three others stopped too; there was that rustle that comes from trying to staunch excited breathing. I didn't dare look around.

The coach scratched his long head with the eraser-end of his pencil. "Tell me your name, age, and class in school."

"Petra Angelica Worshafter. I'm eight and in Frau Beitermeyer's class."

"Frau Beitermeyer?"

"Grade three," I corrected.

The coach nodded and flipped over some pages on the clipboard.

"Peti," I heard Franzel whisper behind me, "this isn't going to be any fun. Let's leave and you can look for me."

"Take this to the doctor's table, please, Fräulein Petra," the coach directed, handing over an index card.

I glanced back over my shoulder. Franzel, standing right behind Ilse now, was looking down at his damp black socks, not at me. That he was wiggling his toes—first the right foot, then the left, like they were having a silly conversation, made me giggle.

"Well, you're a happy child, aren't you?" said the doctor, taking my card. "You're going to do quite well, Petra Angelica." He turned me around and ran his fingers down along my spine. "Now raise your hands above your head. Hold them there."

I stared at the wall while he prodded my back and shoulders. "Lower them, Petra Angelica," he finally instructed. "And look at me."

I lifted my chin and a small fierce light shone into my eyes.

"Watch my finger, don't look away," said the doctor, passing his right index finger between my face and the light. With each pass, his finger darkened. He moved it back and forth, breaking the glare so many times that my eyes started to tear.

"Tell him about the red team," Ilse rasped from behind me.

"Follow my finger, please," said the doctor sharply. After another pass, he clicked off the light.

I blinked. He was completely blackened now, from his head on down. I couldn't see his eyes, his mustache, or even the metal buttons on his jacket. I turned and a bloated yellow circle swam over Ilse and blocked her from view. Circles of various sizes floated silently all through the gymnasium. Here and there a grey, faded child would burst through a circle as if through a gelatin hoop.

"Sit down at the table," continued the charred doctor. "I'll talk to you after I finish with the next few applicants. It's not much to worry about; you just won't be able to do anything that demands perfect peripheral vision. I'll give you a note and you'll take it with you to the next station. For now, take that chair—the other's mine—that's right." Then he stepped stiffly into the yellow orb where Ilse had been.

I shut my eyes. When I opened them, the doctor—pink-skinned again in the cleared air—was squinting into the bleachers above Franzel's head. "One minute," he muttered. He raised an index card and called, "Herr Böhm, may I consult with you?"

As soon as the doctor's back was turned, Franzel slid over to the table. He placed his palms on a sheaf of papers and leaned toward me. "I thought we agreed on the blue team," he said reproachfully. "What do you care about Ilse Kohler?"

"You," the coach's voice rang out. "Volkmann!"

Franzel's hands flew up off the papers as though burned. Wide-eyed, he swiveled about.

"Go and stand behind the line," I whispered. "Hurry up."

The coach and the doctor came striding across the room. "Volkmann," the coach shouted again. He gave a blast on his whistle and suddenly everything and everyone in the gymnasium came to a halt.

"Even if the mother is Aryan," the doctor was saying, "the father isn't. It says so on this card."

"But the card also says he goes to this school."

"That's your headache. The father's just some Jew printer, so what is all this?"

In the stilled gymnasium, someone jumped off something—off the horse—and the air shook.

The doctor stopped right where he was. "I can't see this boy," he said, pointing his index finger.

I started to giggle. Franzel was right there, in full view. He was a small, white-faced boy with brown hair, in a red sweater and dark woolen trousers and dark socks. He was even more visible than anyone else because he was standing on a painted line all by himself. He was standing on that line, clear as life. "Peti," he mouthed silently, turning his eyes to me.

I was still giggling. I said, "He's not really invisible."

"I don't want to see you in here again, Volkmann," the coach said.

"Petra Angelica," said the doctor, brushing past Franzel, "let me explain to you about your eye."

"And in front of us men, men, men, brightly colored, grey, brown, a torrent lasting an hour and twenty minutes. . . . One seemed to see only a few types recurring again and again, but there were between twenty-two and twenty-five thousand different faces! . . . What must Hitler feel when he sees the hundred thousand people whom he summoned, to whom he gave a national soul, people who are ready to die for him. Not only metaphorically speaking but in bitter earnest?"

—the diary of Luise Solmitz

The Parade

THAT MORNING, I awoke feeling I was still marching. Before
I opened my eyes, I felt—stomach down on the mattress,
Mattilde's arm flung high on the pillow against mine—that
I was being put through my paces. The trumpet was vibrat-
ing my lips, my elbows were close-in at my sides, and at the
downbeat: *Turn right!* In truth, I was lying dead as a board,
but I was caught up in the sensation of remembered activity.
Muscle memory, it's called.

For five hours the night before, Kreiswald's Citizens' Band
had practiced marching maneuvers for Passau's Appreciation Day Parade. The event, the first to which our band
would travel, was to celebrate Germany's annexation of Poland as well as the new friendship treaty just signed with
Russia. Posters were everywhere for *A Day of Appreciation
for Our New Land and New Friends.* Bright red letters
spelled out the names of the three participating bands:
Passau, Landau, Kreiswald. The problem was that, except
for our own Founders' Day, when we'd follow a ribbon-hung
police commander's car slowly around Grubenplatz, we of

Kreiswald weren't a true marching band. We were used to playing music from the sitting position—from chairs set on an outdoor platform or the stage in the civic auditorium. A parade through a neighboring city would be, well, quite a change. But Stefan Worshafter had pledged our participation; and since he was the leader, the band rose to its feet.

Worshafter tirelessly exhorted us across the school's frozen playing field. Earlier, in a filter of sunlight, students had practiced there with their youth groups. No wonder the children were so fervent about their after-hours drills. For with the barrel-chested Worshafter in front of us, his black baton barely visible in the darkness, we became not a band of managers and deliverymen and teachers, but something fantastic—something loud and demanding. Who doesn't love being consumed in that way, as one atom in a beautiful, well-defined body? Not for me a leader's isolation and the responsibilities that brings. No, those few meters of mud separating the lawyer Worshafter from our front line—five flutes and two piccolos—were nothing I wanted to breach.

I'd joined the Citizens' Band for, well, the camaraderie, and because I was afraid. All around me our little town was dressed up and shouting—all of Germany was dressed up and shouting. And I stood out because I didn't make one sound at all. I had to find some part, just some sweet little part, in all the excitement. The rest of it—well, to be truthful, I shuddered to think of the rest of it.

So, I resolved to take up the trumpet again. And the vibrations of my lost boyhood surged through me. I was in tune. I was in uniform. I was a participant. That's it. I made music. What peace of mind playing second trumpet brought!

In the third hour of our night drill, the wind died completely and the snow began to tumble straight down in a long velvet curtain that couldn't be batted aside. The flakes clung to our cold faces and fingers. Worshafter shouted: "Follow me! Watch, men, watch what I'm doing! Flutes, keep to formation!"

The session headed toward its fourth hour. Individually at first, then in twos and threes, the lights went out in the buildings surrounding the field; still we didn't stop our maneuvers. We couldn't. Finally, Worshafter dropped his arms and slowly turned. There was always that moment of surprise, seeing his face, not his back. He blinked his black eyes, exhausted. His face was pale and, in a rough, plain way, aging. Some members of the band started clapping; for a second I thought they only meant to keep the circulation going in their hands, but the applause swelled throughout the rows. "Worshafter!" shouted a man from the back. "Worshafter!" "Worshafter!" After a moment, even more people shouted it. Embarrassed a little, I did, too. But my second shout, in truth, felt wonderful—it was wonderful to join in again, not with some instrument, but with my own naked voice.

Our leader beamed at us. "Kreiswald will be proud," he said, and in a voice full of excitement he promised that in Passau we wouldn't be confined to one muddy field, we'd have street after street. Then he pulled his shoulders back a bit more. Slowly, he raised his baton. "Kreiswald!" he shouted with a straight-armed salute.

I returned home just before midnight with my lips numb and nose dripping. My back, too, was stiff. It was nothing that a sip of schnapps and a warm bed wouldn't cure. When she saw me in this condition, Mattilde turned and groaned "Poor Ernst!" into her pillow.

"Don't worry," I told her. "After a day of paperwork at the factory, it's good to have some exercise." With a laugh, I climbed under the sheets. "Now I'm as tough as a soldier."

"My soldier," whispered Mattilde, snuggling into me. "You and Georg, both."

I paused. "Well, it's not much, what I do. I just march, the same as everyone else in the band." I was surprised by my wife's pairing of my name with my son's. Georg's army unit had just been sent to the eastern front. It was his first time away from us. When we finally received a letter, he wrote that things were still calm so he hadn't had to fire his rifle yet, and that he was proud to hear of all I was doing. I had to bite my lip to keep from crying and embarrassing myself. Him—proud of me? When he was the one sticking his neck out? On the bottom of the letter Mattilde was writing back to him, I hastily added a postscript: *Keep far back in the lines, Georg, promise me!*

Mattilde sighed, "I wish I could leave work and go to Passau tomorrow, Ernst."

"Well, it's all right. I'm only in the visitor's band. And, really, you might not be able to see me, anyway. The whole excitement about this Appreciation Day, well—"

"Still, I wish I could be there." She pressed against me. "Let's go to sleep."

"Sweet dreams, Mattilde." Exhausted, I closed my eyes.

Then in what seemed no time at all I was outside again. In uniform, in the forest-green cloth and yellow braid of Kreiswald, I hurried through the early morning streets, negotiating the piles of snow already tromped on by others' boots.

The bus was idling at Grubenplatz with a *Kreiswald Citizens' Band* banner taped to its side. Someone had painted two big swastikas cavorting like acrobats at each end. Above the banner, the row of windows was opaque with frost, although grey circles—peepholes—were slowly appearing down the line. As I got closer, I could see not only the fingers working at clearing the glass, but also, dead-center, the occasional wide eye.

Lifting my trumpet case in a visual reveille, I climbed aboard.

"Gelber," called the trombone, Schloss, thumping the back of the seat in front of him, "here you go. First seat."

"Am I the last to get here?" I turned around. "It looks like everyone's already on board."

"You'd do better to look again."

Craning, I took a quick census of the instruments and overcoats. "But where is Herr Worshafter?"

Joseph Schloss shook his large grey head in the sorrowful way of a teacher who now has to lead his student on to an unwelcome phase in his education. "Herr Worshafter," he said slowly, "is ill. Apparently, he couldn't even get out of bed. Opendorf delivered the message about fifteen minutes ago. He said we're to proceed without him."

I stared at Schloss as if he were mad. "Without—? No. Everything depends on him."

He shifted in his seat and brought up from beneath it the leader's long black baton. I had never seen it this closely. It was metal, a good meter and a half long, with the heft of a birch whipping rod. "Gelber," continued Schloss in his professorial voice, "since you're the first of the second trumpets, we've decided this baton passes to you."

"To me?" I stared at him.

"You're second trumpet," Schloss repeated.

"Why me?"

"You're not that important. You're up on things, in a way, but more dispensable than some of the rest of us. We were unanimous."

"No." My throat closed. "No. What do I know about being the leader, tell me that? I don't know all the parts, or the order of the songs, or the route, or the first steps to our drills."

"I'm sure you know everything. And as for the drill order,

just look at your sheet music and you can tell what comes next. Ernst, you have to do this. You coordinate a great deal of the activity at Brunschenfeld, don't you?"

"But it's a factory. We make boots. Boots and belts and watchstraps, not music."

"The concentration needed is probably much the same," he soothed, reaching over the seat.

The bus lurched into gear. Thrown off-balance, I fell backward, and instinctively my fingers closed on Schloss' wrist. Immediately, he raised the baton. My arm rose with it.

"On to victory," he cried. "The torch is passed. Our leader—Herr Gelber!"

The others roared. After all the drills and practice, the band was not going to be denied the parade.

At noon, when we pulled into Passau and parked under the long, flapping banner proclaiming the town center Jew-free, I was faint with dizziness. Oh, I was sorry I had ever been eager to leave my warm bed. As the players filed past, I stayed in my seat. A good number clapped me on the shoulder, some with a word or two of encouragement, and I couldn't trust myself to respond. But when Helmut Frasier came down the aisle, tapping his drumsticks along the tops of the seats, I pulled him down next to me. "Please, the truth," I whispered. "Tell me if the snares, well, really look to Worshafter to set the beat."

He sat back and eyed me warily. "I don't know what you mean."

I leaned closer. "Which instrument is in charge? Which one, drums or baton?"

"You can't be serious," he said.

"I am. You think this is a joke?"

With a slight shake of his head, Frasier began to get up.

"No." Frantic, I grabbed the sticks out of his hand. "I need to know! You have to tell me."

"Ernst!" He wrenched them back. "Control yourself, all right?" Frasier sat down. His lips tightened. "All right," the banker said slowly. "It depends."

I waited.

He cleared his throat. "Actually, we can't always tell what Worshafter wants. He's so far in front of us. Sometimes we can't see the baton, or he's gone around a corner before we have." Frasier looked over his shoulder. "At those times, we guess and decide what to do so we don't look like fools. We speed up, or slow down. Whatever."

"The bass drum, too? You mean all of you do this?"

The banker nodded, chin against his chest.

I exhaled. "Thank you, Helmut." I felt relieved, as if I'd just been readmitted to the corps. "Please tell the other drums that it's the same with me, I'm not in charge. As soon as I lower the baton for the first beat, the drums will take over. You'll set the pace and keep setting it. No one else in the band has to know."

His face drained of color. "You're supposed to be in charge."

"But you just admitted that you didn't watch for Worshafter's cues."

"Don't you play second trumpet?" he demanded, the wattle under his chin shaking. "Don't you know about counting out the beat?"

The bus driver shifted clumsily on his perch. "Aren't you two getting off with the others?"

"One minute." Lowering my voice, in a tone as calm and rational as I could make it, I continued, "A trumpet doesn't play all the time, the drums do. There've been whole stretches where I've just held my trumpet flat to my chest, listening to the music like I was a bystander." I paused. "Tell your group to do what they've always done—only now just do it louder. So I can hear it from the front. I'll be mimicking what you send out as best I can."

"But you know the drums are supposed to follow. That's why we're behind everyone else. Understand?"

Someone was rapping on my window from outside. Clearing a circle on the glass, I could make out Hauptbaum, the younger one, the pharmacist, not the one in accounting who until last year had been married to an old schoolmate of Mattilde's. Elon Simon, her name had been before her marriage. A Jewess. "Please come out here, Herr Gelber," the younger Hauptbaum shouted as my breath again whitened about him. "There's a man here you should speak with."

I clasped Frasier's hand. "I've got to meet someone. Maybe he's a substitute. Maybe you can forget all this. I have to go." Seizing the baton, I made a quick descent from the bus into the fresh air. Across the plaza groups of men were huddled together. My marching companions, the line of first and second trumpets—I could hear the hesitant, infant bursts of their tuning up. Joyfully, I started toward them.

But the younger Hauptbaum waved me over, gesturing with his clarinet at the resplendent stranger to his left. With a firm chin and sound bearing, the man wore his gold uniform as a prince might: aware of its effect on his onlookers, but seeming to care about that not one jot. "Oswold Kenninski," younger Hauptbaum called. "From our host-band."

The man smiled and raised a pale, ornately carved walking stick, oddly rubber-tipped. "I salute you, Herr Gelber."

I hurried over, slipping between two flapping flags. "It's much too premature for that. I hope Herr Hauptbaum, here, explained to you—"

"You're the new leader, yes. I've already sent a note to the announcer about the change." Kenninski shrugged away anything further I might say by reaching into a brown leather pouch which he wore strapped diagonally across his chest. He was a handsome man of about fifty. "Here is the order of events for the celebration. The parade, as usual, of course, will come first. After that, we'll have speeches and all the rest. It's going to be a full day."

Out of the corner of my eye, I saw Frasier whispering to some of the other drummers; it was the lawyer contingent—Lizzmer, Opendorf and Schenkel. The four of them were standing in a circle, drums centermost, sticks crossed atop the rims. Their heads tilted together, no nodding, no visible disagreements. I had to get over there, to confirm what had to be done.

With a sigh, I took the mimeographed sheet. "So the parade will begin in twenty minutes?"

"Oh no," he said, his eyes widening, "in about eight. You'd better reset your watch if you expect to start off the parade for us."

"Start this?" I laughed, I didn't believe it.

"Herr Gelber, Passau accorded Kreiswald the honor of leading the Parade of Appreciation in its invitation. Kreiswald accepted. It is our honor to have you start off everything."

"I didn't know."

He gave me a smile. "We have perfect confidence in your capabilities."

"But certainly you can imagine—" I began, then I saw his jaw set with the challenge and I stopped. "You must, well, imagine." Behind me, the trumpets were tuning each other and each lighthearted trill, each blended note only underscored my growing distress.

"I'm sorry? I must have missed the end of your sentence."
He leaned forward slightly.

I took a breath and in the rush of the exhalation said, "You
would do my city the greater honor if you would march at
my side this afternoon, through Passau. If you would lead
with me."

Kenninski threw back his head with a laugh. "Me? I don't
march. Did you think that I do? Herr Gelber, I'm on the
review platform with the mayor and the speakers and the
police commandant. When such things mattered, my family
had a *von* before our name. We're an old lineage."

"You must understand," I burst out, "I belong in the ranks.
I'm not a leader, I know nothing about it. If the marchers
take my instruction, it's all lost."

He grimaced. "Lower your voice. Do you know who's
standing behind me?"

I turned. Göring's pugnacious profile swam into view.
The general was talking to a well-fed, grey-haired man in a
beautiful dark blue wool coat. "Are you proposing we au-
thorize your company to make this new product?" asked
Göring.

I spun about on my heel. Kenninski fixed his gaze on my
face as if this would keep his words from sliding past me.
"You have to start the parade," he continued grimly. "The
order has been set. First the Kreiswald band, then the
schoolchildren from Landau, the Bensheim band, then our
schoolchildren—the schools have been preparing for weeks.
Then our band, last. Last is the Passau band, as host." He
jabbed his stick down at the pavement. It sprang back,
smack into the center of his gloved palm.

I nodded, trying to keep my attention fastened on him,
though every ounce of my body was straining to get away.
It was no use. I lifted my eyes and Fritz Vogel, the silver
glockenspiel gleaming before him, passed by and waved to

me. He had the startled stare of a new father, which indeed he was. "Isn't this town something?" he shouted.

Said Kenninski, "Time is short. I have other duties to perform and other people to contact. I'll have to take—"

The snares erupted with the harsh staccato of machine guns and cut off the rest of his sentence. Was it a message, the drums had reached a consensus? I spun about but could see no one I knew, not on the plaza. These drummers wore uniforms of brown and gold. Just men from Bensheim loosening up their wrists. And when I turned back around, I saw Vogel walking away.

"Herr Kenninski," called a girlish voice. "We must get you to the stand with the other notables."

"Well, there you are." He clapped me on the shoulder. "Time's less than short—it's gone. There's nothing else to do for it now."

Suddenly, it was true. The town square was taken over by movement, everything lengthening, stretching. Where before there'd been isolated groups of band members, hunch-shouldered, now I saw several long lines weaving in a sort of continuous body, arms and legs rippling. Disparate sounds: flugelhorn, cymbals, and such had begun to blend in one excited murmur. There was a humming one felt not just low in the throat, but deeper, in the stomach. Boots were not lifted high and placed firmly heel-down—that would come later—they shuffled like slippers, quietly across the bricks. From some other street, further back than this ring of buildings, a police siren pulsated. In the center of the plaza, the loudspeakers sent out a stream of static, but no voice yet, no one insisting we were to begin.

"Gelber," said Kenninski, "you have to go now."

"I'm afraid—I'm afraid I'm ill."

"You're not." He took his hand from my shoulder.

"Herr Kenninski?" cried the woman, her voice much fainter, "are you coming?"

His eyes darted past me. "Where in the world—?"

The loudspeaker sputtered and a cheer went up, filling the air.

Kenninski grimaced, still searching. "All these good people—ah, there! God, what a beauty." Lifting his walking stick over his head in a glorious straight-armed sweep, he called out, "Fräulein Kirschener!"

Instinctively, I turned, too. The crowd was pressed behind the ropes cordoning off the plaza. They stood at the sides, and there were so many of them with their arms in the air: fur-clad or cloth, gloved or bare-handed. One of these arms had to be gesturing to Herr Kenninski, but I couldn't make out which. The rest were trying to get the attention of the brown-and-gold Bensheim band, or of the children gathering under the banners of their youth groups. Names filled the air. "Ruthe! Ruthe Pfeizer, look, I came. I see you." "Robert Schmidt, here!" "I'm here, Therese—your Grandma Neurath." "Fritz Posner. Thomas Posner. Boys!" If Mattilde had been free to leave work, would she be waving me on, too?

"Look to the right." Kenninski's voice was hot in my ear. "See her? From one of Passau's most prominent families. Munitions. Three factories, with a new one just going up in Poland. Do you see her?" He pointed the rubber tip, singling out a red coatsleeve, a glove with its long, black, elegant fingers, regally still. The one arm in the crowd not waving, but waiting.

"Fräulein!" He clicked his heels. With a clear smile, he set off.

I grabbed him. "Wait, what about me? Where should I go?"

"To the front." He gestured to the right of the loudspeakers. "To the head."

"But, well, what's the parade route? I have no idea of the way."

"Don't worry," he said, tweaking my arm, "you'll be able to tell. Good luck, Herr Gelber." Then he turned and was absorbed into the crowd.

Fearful to be left standing there, nowhere, with the leader's black baton in my hand, I cut between Bensheim's rows of trombones and trumpets, in the direction Kenninski had indicated. At the front at least there'd be faces I knew: Schloss, Vogel, younger Hauptbaum—and the rest, all in formation. Oh, Frasier, be there.

The loudspeakers were booming. "One Leader! One People! One Victory! For bringing into the fold the outlaw state of Poland, and in honor of the new treaty with Russia—long may both prosper!—we hereby commence the celebration of this, our Day of Appreciation. In appreciation, all here today . . ."

Kreiswald's green and yellow uniforms were before me, their backs to me. The last line, the drummers' line, was—in reverse—first.

Said the loudspeakers: "Participating in Passau's great event are the towns of Landau, Bensheim . . ."

"Helmut?"

Frasier turned, horrified. "Go," he rasped, prodding me with his stick. "To the front. Hurry."

I ran. I placed myself three meters before the flutes and piccolos as the loudspeakers announced, ". . . honor of Kreiswald. We turn our parade over to their leader, Herr Ernst Gelber. Herr Gelber, as you wish, you may begin!"

The speaker system was clicked off.

On the bricked streets across the stone plaza there was

silence. The *Jew-Free* banner over the bus fluttered once and grew still. Further in, the circle of red flags sank in slow succession against their poles, the black swastikas hidden. The crowd was turned toward me, their faces clear. Their puffs of breath curled in the winter air. One little girl, balanced atop perhaps her mother's shoulders, started to weep. The tears made their way down her pink, pink cheeks and rounded chin. She wasn't wearing a hat, stupidly unprotected on a day like today. "Ba ba," she sobbed, grabbing in both fists the woman's brown wispy hair. "Ba ba."

Frightened, I glanced down at my boots. They were drenched in the pond of my shadow.

"Now," I heard.

I looked back up.

Tilting out from the crowd was a toothless old man. He was so stooped, his chin quivered against the cluster of Great War medals pinned to his coat. "Where's your son?" he hissed.

A shiver ran through me. Was he asking about Georg?

"Where's your song?" He spoke louder. "Lead it off, I'm waiting. Now." Despite his wasted appearance, he lifted his arms with a tensile strength.

Obediently I followed his movements; I raised the black baton.

The bass drum thudded in a distant explosion. The snares. The report of my beloved trumpets, the trombones, flutes, piccolos, the baritone horns—the full barrage. At once the ground trembled—all those feet, marching in place.

The crowd cheered. "To new lands, new friends!" Their arms went up. Why, they were showing me the route, they were pulling me forward. And from behind, setting the pace, came those deep loud cracking sounds. The thunder had started and it wouldn't stop now, for behind it was another front line, and another—and another, and groups of children prepared to turn cartwheels in the few sudden clearings, and more flags waving, and more bursts of thunder. Lined up to the horizon, the crowd nearly sang. How they wanted this parade to come toward them!

Well, I saw I could please them. I took a step, my arm pumping, a great leader.

"The prolific German mother is to be accorded the same place of honor in the German Volk community as the combat soldier, since she risks her body and her life for the people and the Fatherland as much as the combat soldier does in the roar and thunder of battle." With these words, Reich Physician Leader Dr. Wagner, head of the People's Health Section in the Reich leadership of the party, at the behest of the Führer, announced the creation of a Medal of Honor for prolific German mothers at the Party Day of Labor.

Three million German mothers, on the German Mother's Day in 1939, for the first time will be solemnly awarded the new badge of honor by the leaders of the party. These celebrations are to be held every year on Mother's Day and on the Awarding of Medals Day for prolific mothers.

—the *Völkischer Beobachter*
December 25, 1938

The Trespasser

"WHAT IS THAT?" I sat up in bed. "Rolf, I hear someone trying to break in."

"Into the police commander's house? Impossible. Go back to sleep, little one, you have nothing to fear."

Reluctantly, I lay back down and turned toward him. In the darkness, the contours of his face shifted and he looked different. One of his eyes, the one not pressed against the pillow, was watching me.

He said, "Gerda, count to ten. If you still hear something after that, I'll go outside and check."

"One."

"Go on."

I continued counting under my breath. As I did, his eye closed and his face was familiar again. His breathing was slow and persuasive. *Nine.* I kissed the tip of my finger and touched it to his nose. *Ten.*

"Ten," I said aloud, but quietly. No sound anywhere in the world but his light snoring. After a moment, I moved my legs, tried to get comfortable after the dinner I hadn't much wanted to eat—food hadn't been sitting well with me recently. Perhaps it was all the ersatz ingredients we had to use—the usual staples were no longer always available. But that couldn't be all of it. I could still taste that chestnut soufflé Rolf had urged upon me at dinner. Not only was it made from real eggs and the full amount of sugar but it was also, he said, a gift from a new colleague. I hadn't managed to get down more than a mouthful; happily, he gobbled up the rest.

With a sigh, I shifted around on the mattress. Through the half-open window the branches of the apricot tree, full of buds and newly burst leaves, shook slightly. Spring made it shake. Spring made everything shake.

Tugging at my cotton nightgown, I swung my legs out of bed.

Suddenly Rolf's arm thumped down, across my right thigh. "Where are you going?"

"The window." I jumped back, heart beating.

The cover slid like a blue sheet of ice off his bare chest. He sat up. "Can't be—" he gasped. Without taking his white eyes from my face, he leaned over and slid open the drawer to the nightstand.

Though the gun was barely limned in the sheenless dark, I glanced quickly away.

His voice was quiet. "I'll take care of this. You stay still."

I paused. "I just thought the air would be sweet."

But he was out of bed, and already moving toward the window. I couldn't hear him crossing the room. I strained. How could I have thought I could hear someone trying to break in, someone coming from even further away, if I couldn't even hear him walking a few meters off?

"Rolf, stop. I just wanted to get some fresh air."

He turned around; his left shoulder and arm were silhouetted against the window, part of the apricot tree now. The branches were shaking their way out of his body. "What? Repeat yourself, Gerda."

"I just—"

He took a step closer to me, and more fully in front of the glass. Suddenly the tree moved all around him but its movement was awful, a kind of St. Vitus's Dance. Branches became arms twitching in a network of veins; the spring buds blackened like clots. It was a swirl of death and Rolf was caught up in it.

Horrified, I looked away. "Outside, I heard something outside, I think," I said, and my hand went to the open V-neck of my nightgown. "Get out of here—please, find him."

He didn't move, not one step from the window. "Gerda," he murmured, from the midst of the tangle. That was his head—that round shadow they were grabbing.

I choked down my nausea. "Maybe I should—should I go home to my flat?" Before I could get out another word, I leaned over the bed and retched.

"My God, little one." Rolf was holding my head between his hands—between one of his hands and the gun. The metal cold against my feverish skin, and pressing, hurt me, too.

I clawed for his wrist. "Put that down, Rolf."

"My God." He was aghast.

My hair fell forward as he let go. I didn't have time to brush the ends out of the way. I heaved again.

When, quivering, I slowly sat back up, I felt naked. I gathered the sheet up around me and sank against the pillows. My hair hung in damp chilly cords against my neck. "Water." I shut my eyes.

He said from a few meters away, "Fine, right, that's good. Now just one moment, I need some light."

"Don't—the air raids."

"I *know* that, Gerda. Besides, there won't be a raid, not with our flak gunners." This time, I could hear his every move. There was the *snap* of the blackout blind pulled down hard against the sill, then he was thudding back across the room. He flicked on the small lamp on his way to the sink.

I kept my eyes closed; I didn't want to see anything I couldn't explain, I wanted only to forget what had just happened in front of the window. The branches changing to arms and grabbing him—that was only a distortion brought about by the dark. Not real the way, say, a haircut was real. The rush of water stopped.

"Here, take this glass." He stood near the bed, holding a small goblet. Even in the dim haze of lamplight, I could see how a flush covered his neck and much of his chest. He was sweating, and the line of black hairs that started under the waistband of his undershorts and continued spreading gracefully outward up to his collarbone glistened damply.

I took the glass, but didn't sip from it. Everything was confused inside me.

"No one is out there," said Rolf. "We're fine."

My eyes flicked over to the window. The oilcloth shade hung straight down. Nothing, no breeze puffed behind it.

"You have to stop acting on impulse. You let fear rule you and look at the result."

"I'm sorry. Maybe I *should* go back to the flat."

He shot me a sidelong look. "Stay, Gerda." He wiped his white shins and feet with a small towel. "The truth is I blame myself for everything."

"No," I blurted, my mouth dry, "you haven't done anything wrong, you know you haven't."

"My little one," he murmured, "I love you, too." He studied the small braided rug that had caught most of the damage, then he sucked in his breath and knelt down.

"Rolf, stop, don't do that."

"My hands are already dirty."

"I don't care, you shouldn't—please, let me."

But he continued to roll up the brown oval, turning over the wet fibers with his blunt fingers. When he stood, in his hands, contained as neatly as possible, was the mess I'd just made. "No one," he said, his jaw working, "can break into this house. You're the safest woman in Kreiswald. You believe that I won't let anyone hurt you, don't you?"

I nodded and leaned back against the headboard.

"Try to rest. I won't be long." When he turned around, there was a dark streak of sweat in the crease of his shorts.

I shut my eyes. I must have dozed off. From the distance came the wail of a police siren. Somehow, its very persistence calmed me down. Over and over it started up, wailed, subsided, yet no matter how far it traveled in one direction or the other it never completely stopped. In my sleep, I seemed to follow it, that threaded, mewling sound.

A while later there was silence. I remember my arms rising over my head; a film, a sheath slipping away; a breeze curling around me. It was delightful. Then, the whisper: "Gerda, my Gerda, my Gerda." The hot nap of a cloth rubbing and licking my face, my neck, between my breasts, the damp tangle of hairs under my arms, and further down. The siren started up again. I tried to hold on to it. Against its muffled pulsation, someone cried out: *You! Wait!* A series of sharp, popping sounds. Someone, far away. My legs—then everything—shaking.

One shred, one red tissue of dawn, opened up behind the apricot branches. It floated there as if pinned while the clouds turned from grey to mottled blue and white around it. When had he gotten up and opened the blind?

"Rolf?" I sat up. I felt graceless—bloated and emptied out at the same time. My nightgown lay on the floor; I didn't want to bend down to retrieve it. "Sweetheart," I called again through a sour-tasting mouth.

Reaching for the edge of the nightstand, I rose unsteadily to my feet and from there went slowly over to the window for some air. Below, through the clustered blooms, a familiar brown uniform; he seemed to be leaning against the bars of the wrought iron fence, near the latched gate. "How long have you been outside?" I waved.

He hurried over to the house and looked up between the green branches. Then he saw me, as pink as I was. "Satan Christus," he muttered.

"Oh!" I ducked behind the wall. The wide face beneath the police cap wasn't Rolf's.

"You must excuse me, please excuse me, Frau—" None of the men in the station knew what to call me. Frau Terskan wasn't correct. And although Frau Stella *was*—well, they knew Torgood or had at least heard about him: how he'd been transferred to Passau while his wife pretended to live in a small rented flat but often spent the night in Commander Terskan's house. But with all that information, they didn't know everything. They couldn't. Not even the best of the police could know everything.

"Excuse me, Frau—" the officer repeated haplessly.

"Go away! Leave."

In the pause, the oilcloth shade fluttered by my head, then the stranger called, almost gently, "I'm posted here until eight. After that, another guard's coming." He waited a moment. "I've been on duty since two in the morning when Commander Terskan called. Everything's been fine, there's been nothing irregular. No one will bother you."

I stood pressed against the cool grey wall. To reach out a bare arm to pull down the blackout shade would be an admission that he had seen all he thought he had. "Shouldn't you be at the fence? Would you return to your post, please?"

A click of heels. "Right away, gnädige Frau."

I waited, then slid away, one hand at my breasts, the other

THE TRESPASSER   125

covering my private parts. The posture was silly but instinc-
tive. The guard couldn't see in and he wouldn't dare lift his
eyes now; still, he was out there, with a picture in his mind
that we both knew showed me naked and embarrassed. Why
hadn't Rolf told me he was posting a guard? This was just
like him, wasn't it—shielding me from knowing what was
going on.

I tossed the edge of the sheet back onto the bed. Everything was a mess. In the last few weeks the simple rituals of
romance that had relieved me of my dreary past had begun
to feel dreary themselves. The phone call where he'd say in
a low rough voice: *I'm sending the car by;* the angle he
would tilt my head up for a kiss upon greeting; how we'd
enter Kaski's Restaurant and, backs straight, go toward the
table with the blue curtain around it, which of course only
made us as visible as it made us discreet; the tiny gift boxes
I'd unwrap on the twenty-third of each month—seven of
them, so far.

But posting someone in the back courtyard, and only for
show! The guard was a pretense. Rolf *knew* no one could
break into the commander's house. I knew it, too, really,
after my first burst of fear. I could see right through his
intentions by now. No doubt we were coming to know each
other quite well.

I bent for my nightgown and shivered. The gown was still
damp. From its folds came the sickly-sweet odor of vomit.
With a shudder of nausea, I threw it back down. But it was
too late: gagging, hands over my mouth, I ran for the bath-
room. I made it to the sink and let go.

Afterward, when I finally lifted my chin to the mirror, I
saw through the film of tears not one bleary blond head, but
two: one was wavering, peeking childishly in and out from
the side of the other. I tried to smile, but the effect was
dismal and at last the second head faded. "Gerda"—gingerly

I touched my flat belly; it felt tight as a drum—"you know it. You're pregnant." With a cry, I leaned over the sink again.

There was no use in waiting. I'd never gotten anywhere by waiting.

I walked down the alley. A black van, with all but the driver's windows painted over, was idling in back of the police station, its tailpipe rattling against the back bumper. I edged past it and, as quickly as I could, made my way to the front of the building.

It was a long time ago, when I'd last pulled open that door. I took a deep breath.

Hitting me first was the warm, waxy smell of leather. To either side, along the benches, a dozen officers were hunched over, cleaning black, knee-high boots and something else—holsters. There were rows of boots and holsters to be polished.

"Where," I blurted, "is Commander Terskan?"

The man to my left made his rag crack like a pistol shot across a boot before looking up. "Oh," he mumbled, getting to his feet. Then his gaze flickered to the back of the room. Behind the abandoned main desks, just opposite the wall of file cabinets, a door was open, and I could hear Rolf's voice echoing up from the bottom of a deep stairwell. "—you hear me?" he was saying, "stop it. Get control of yourself." Then footsteps, climbing.

Karl Prudmann came through the door. Like a man only half-awake he looked around the bright room as if trying to find something or someone familiar—as if only then would he be willing to keep moving. He blinked; his wide, pale eyes settled on me. And blinked again. He made an attempt to straighten his shoulders but he seemed utterly bowed.

"Now you have the forms to fill out." Rolf cut behind him. He didn't see me; he was concentrating on massaging his upper right arm. "Next time I'll send a second man with you, in case another prisoner tries something stupid like that again. This one should have been in physical restraints from the start. I don't like prying them off me."

"Frau Stella," Karl Prudmann mumbled.

With the grace of movement sometimes only a large man has, Rolf swung about. "Ah"—and he gestured toward his chair—"a surprise. It's been a very long time since you've visited us." His tone was pleasantly formal. He swiveled the chair around so that my back was to Prudmann's desk.

It was more unsettling to be inside the station than I'd thought. Even the sound of the shoeshine brushes whisking against the hollow boots and long straps made me nervous. I sat down and quickly leaned forward: "What's the matter with your arm? Why are you rubbing it?"

"Gerda," murmured Rolf, bending toward me, his face caught between severity and teasing, "have you come to ask about my health? Why are you here? Are you still feeling ill from last night?"

"I brought you a present." And I placed a small package wrapped in brown butcher paper atop a stack of cardboard folders. "I have another one for you, too."

"Where is it?"

"It's hidden. Aren't you going to open this one?"

He glanced over his shoulder and said quietly, "No, I want what you're keeping back from me. Where is it? You know I'll ferret it out." His hand rested next to the package, fingertips brushing the double-knotted string.

The typewriter had started up behind me. Each keystrike stuttering, fretful. Did all clerks type in this awful way? "Can't we go outside to talk?" I whispered. "I'm pregnant."

He swept the little box with its gift of cuff links off the stack of folders and picked up one of the files. With a grimace, he flipped it open. The front door banged open; the hard heels of boots, going quickly down the outside steps; then the *slam* shut. Without looking up, he muttered, "I'll meet you near the collection box in the park. It's best if you leave just as you came in. Ten minutes, all right?"

By then, as it does in spring, it was raining—but not consistently; the air shifted between mists and watery streams of sun. Rolf's eyes were hidden under the dark visor of his cap. "It's not the best timing, Gerda," he said. He reached into his pocket and tossed a few coins into the collection box for the army's relief fund. "Let's walk."

I kept up with him on the gravel path that bisected the central field with its new bronze statues of infantrymen and factory workers. The tiny swastika-flags surrounding each base hung damply about their poles. Since it was midmorning, Vorchtsbaum Park was nearly abandoned. The mothers were cleaning and shopping at this hour and the lovers were separated until the lunch breaks approved by their jobs.

Rolf headed toward the bridge that led into the linden grove. "You should have taken precautions."

"What are you saying? How—?" My face grew hot. "How could I have used birth control? It's been illegal since the war. Aryans are encouraged, aren't we, by the government to—?"

"Gerda. You know what I mean." He barely paused. "You shouldn't have let me come near you at certain times of the month. You've always been too willing to follow your impulses, without considering the consequences. You couldn't have thought I'd be happy about this, could you, little one?"

"I did. Your first child!"

"It's not."

I stumbled, my hands on my stomach. "What? Rolf, wait."

He already had one foot on the bridge. It was a black-planked, Japanese-like affair that I'd crossed many times.

Now it looked unreal and fragile under his weight, under the single shaft of sunlight that pressed down on its floorboards. Rolf walked a few steps and the stream of yellow light disappeared, only to reappear just as suddenly a bit further on, still pressing on the tilting slick slope in front of him.

"What's happening? You're frightening me!"

At my cry, two huge crows took wing. Rolf turned to face me. The water beads caught in his mustache and eyebrows made him silver-haired; he looked like he'd aged in just the last few moments. Rubbing his right arm, he said, "It's all right, little one."

His boots crunched on the gravel path. A meter away from me, he stopped. "Legally," he said, "it's his first child, it's Torgood's."

"It can't be! And I was careful, as much as it was possible for anyone to be." Then I heard myself say: "I want to divorce him."

Rolf snorted. The mustache hairs directly under his nose were dark again. "Of course, you want to divorce him! You've always wanted to. When all this began, I spoke with a lawyer about it. I had him draw up some papers, so we'd be ready if the situation demanded it."

"You did that?" My voice shook, "Then it's done? That part of my life is finished?"

"If you sign. If you agree to it."

"Do you agree?"

With a tight smile, he took my arm and slid it through his. "Let's cut through the lindens. It's quicker. I can't be away from work any longer."

But I said, "You do want us to get married, don't you?"

"Of course I do," he said. "But this has to be done correctly. When I get back to the station, I'll call the lawyer and tell him you're coming by to initial the papers. It will be very simple."

We continued without speaking through the warm, dripping air. As we entered the black-barked grove, the sun came out. Then the open pasture of the park burst into view between the lindens—the expanse ahead was such a bright yellow-green, it was dazzling. "Oh!" I whispered, stopping right where I was. It seemed impossible to enter the steam rising off the grasses and not dissolve. But strolling through it, ankle-deep, were the first of the lunchtime lovers. They floated through the bright space so casually, tears came to my eyes.

Rolf turned me toward him. Across his face and down his chest fell the shadows of thin black trees. "Who else," he muttered, bending over, his lips warm on my neck, "knows about this baby?"

"No one else."

"Good. I don't want to jeopardize anything at this point." And his hands slid over my stomach. "Little one," he whispered, "stay little. If you start to show too soon, it won't matter who you don't talk to. The child will be marked forever as our bastard. For now, it's important to keep everything strictly inside."

I wiped the perspiration from my upper lip. The lawyer's office stood at the top of three flights of ironwork stairs. Of the eight people scattered among the dozen or so desks in the large main room, only one got up as I entered. The others were much too absorbed with their papers to be curious about another client.

I told the woman my name. "Is Herr Worshafter—?"

A moment later, a stout, energetic man came out of an office fronted with frosted glass. "I'm glad to meet you, Frau Stella. Come in, please." He shut the glass door behind us and rubbed his palm over his bald scalp, to smooth back the few strands. "Commander Terskan telephoned that you'd be

by. Please take a chair. I have the documents right here." He
tapped an open folder on the desk.

"What do I have to do, Herr Worshafter?"

He turned the folder around so that it faced me. "Verify
that the information at the top of this page is correct"—and
he pointed the nub of his fountain pen at the first sheet—
"and initial it, here." He made a faint mark in the corner.
"Then"—he flipped over the page—"read this section and
initial here, at the bottom, and on the third—"

"Yes?" I leaned over, only pretending to scan the densely
typed paragraphs. There were so many ways to be happy,
weren't there? The moment that seems awful and terrifying
is usually the way into a new life. Hadn't I found that out,
time and time again? Bored at school, I found myself suddenly at work in a clothing factory, because of my father's
death. Exhausted by the factory, I found myself suddenly at
a better job a plant nursery. Unhappy in marriage, I found
myself—"I'm sorry, Herr Worshafter, what did you just ask?"

"I was discussing the grounds," he said, a little annoyed.
"On what grounds are you seeking this divorce?"

I sat back blankly. "What are you talking about?"

"The grounds approved by our recent reforms: racially
undesirable partner or racial incompatibility; venereal dis-
ease—excuse me, gnädige Frau." He paused. Then he continued, setting up his rhythm by tapping the ebony pen
against the desk edge. "Refusal to procreate; immorality;
mental illness; a three-year separation; adultery; and eu-
genic weakness. Forgive me for being indiscreet, but which
one applies to Herr Stella?"

I looked at him in alarm. I had no idea I'd have to charge
Torgood with something. I pressed my lips together and
tried to swallow. On the counter behind the lawyer was a
large-bellied metal jug. "Is that water? Do you mind—?"

"Of course not, allow me." The chair squeaked as it swiveled.

"I haven't been feeling well lately."

"There's something going around. My wife is ill, also." He handed me the glass. "I hope you're not upsetting yourself unnecessarily. The legal procedures for divorce are well-established by now, and in personal terms, the damage is behind you. You should focus solely on what you hope to gain."

The water was tepid and tasted faintly of its metal container. "I thought I was only required to write in my initials. Commander Terskan, who's been looking after my welfare, said that everything had been taken care of for me."

Herr Worshafter shrugged with a mock-helpless smile. "A man of the law but no lawyer! The law does have certain niceties it demands of its petitioners. It requires you to make a charge against your spouse. As the wronged party, you know what Herr Stella has done and you can and must state that here." He held up a hand and interrupted himself, "No, let me finish."

He shifted back in his chair. "First, in no way does your making a claim reflect any wrongdoing on your part. Second, if you don't want to reveal what Herr Stella did—if you feel you're trespassing against some, shall I say, personal vows or ethics—you should know that the category you charge him under doesn't have to be precise. Just choose something, and as long as he signs to it, it doesn't matter."

I nodded. "Well, could you, I'm not sure, define immorality for me?"

"Oh, now surely, Frau Stella!" he protested and smiling, he flung his arms wide, palms up. "Do you want me to list the unsavory details for you? Is Herr Stella a homosexual? The State considers that seriously, as quite another matter. Or perhaps a man who you found to be engaging in—"

I said agitatedly, "I really don't want to do this!"

"Well, then we're done. I did think that when the commander telephoned me he said I was to proceed as swiftly as possible, but I must have misunderstood. My error." He reached over for the file.

"Wait. If I do this, how long—?"

"—will the divorce take? If everything goes smoothly, I can move it through the courts quickly, say, six weeks to two months. Otherwise, I'd have to admit a year is more than possible."

"A year from now?" I turned my head in distress. Through the wall of frosted glass the shapes of the workers in the front office flickered. They seemed to be living in another world entirely, one very different from where I sat. Everything about them—their outlines, their colors, even their gestures—seemed muted and impenetrable and distant. I stared, trying to find a mouth or a nose or some tiny, recognizable detail, but I couldn't. Except for Herr Worshafter, whom I'd see if I'd only turn back around, everyone else in the world was there, in the distance on the other side of the glass. Sweat trickled down under my arms. Of all the people in the world, Torgood was the most removed from me; I could barely recall what his face looked like.

"All right," I said. "Adultery."

"Herr Stella committed adultery. You're saying he broke his vows by committing adultery?"

I raised my chin. "Yes," I said. I heard myself say that *yes* and suddenly I was furious. "Yes, he did—more than a dozen times. He thought he was covering it up, but I—it was horrible. There were many late nights, one in particular. It was the last one. He came to our bed still wearing his uniform and he"—the words came fast, as if I'd always known them—"kept moaning in his sleep all night, 'Frau Kauss, dear Ruthe

Kauss! Your throat, your sweet neck!' At least, I think that was the name. We'd had a fight and so—"

Herr Worshafter held up his palm. "No need. The charge alone will do if all goes well." He handed me the black pen.

Quickly I signed my name where he indicated, then I flipped over the sheets and jotted my initials by each of the three faint check marks. I sat back against the hard slats of the chair.

"You must date it, too, please. Each page."

I bit my lip. "I hope," I said, rolling the pen between my fingers, "that she got what she deserved. That Ruthe Kauss was—she was an adulterous whore."

That night, with the guard pacing in the garden below, Rolf and I made love as if we were saying goodbye to my body. Never again would he hold this body—not even now, he whispered, was it Gerda's. Thin, delicate, impulsive Gerda, girl Gerda, with whom he had fallen so fiercely in love. Soon in his arms would be only a mother's body, one harboring—we had our secret—his child. His child, this speck of hardness, of infinitesimal beating fluid flesh inside me where, for all my life, there'd been emptiness—or had it been blood? He shoved my legs apart, and moved me over him, then he, too, was inside. And tried to get in further. To prod the speck to life? To dislodge it? To push it inside more deeply, burying it in my crouching frame?

"Paris," he panted, his hand on my back.

I bent my head. His rough words punctuated by our movements. "We'll go there. Paris. Soon. I promise. You want that, don't you? Now that it's ours, now with the victory, perfume, romance. Our country's, now. You want that? Do you want it?"

It was all I could do not to collapse atop him, as I told him: Yes. Please. Soon.

"Little one." He grabbed me down, to his mouth, stopped my voice with his tongue. My breath fled into his throat.

That week, and the next, *and* the next, the days lengthened; each warm moment nudged the buds and flowers wider. I was dizzy often, from the fragrance in the air and from the craving for foods that I tried not to bring to my mouth; instead of gaining weight, I lost it, and still my waist and hips seemed to widen. Against such persistence, I ate even less. I felt thick and heavy and trapped, and outside Rolf's house—and under the window of my nearly useless flat—came the series of guards. They were still posted against the trespasser and they stood diligently at back fence and front stoop, staring at the line of bushes, the street lamps, the alleyway, hour after hour.

"Good evening, gnädige Frau."

With barely a nod to the current guard, I opened the back gate. That afternoon there'd been a dense, drenching rain, and instead of cleansing the air, the downpour had left it heavy and humid. I knew I was moving too slowly, that it was clear I was pregnant. But out of the corner of my eye, I saw the guard wasn't watching me. He was studying a little boy who was all by himself and not more than a toddler; the child was diligently poking a sharp, broken branch between the iron bars of the fence.

I went up to Rolf's back door and let myself in. He'd said he'd meet me at seven. It was five to the hour. The inside of the house was stuffy. By habit, I went through all the rooms, pulling down the blackout shades for the evening. Then I flicked on a small light by the sofa and opened up the pages of the *Kompass*. *Food Rations to Be Cut,* said the headline. I read the article, then went up to the bedroom.

He was standing at the closed window, looking down through the leaves of the apricot tree. They were a thick, glossy green.

I started. "Rolf, I've been here for twenty minutes, didn't you see me come in?"

He pulled down the blind before turning around. The room went dim, not shadowed but drained. Evenly he said, "He won't sign. Put on the lamp."

I groped for the cord. "What are you talking about?"

"You can't guess? Torgood sent back the papers without a mark on them. He didn't sign them."

"No, are you sure?" The pool of light extended from the nightstand to the edge of the bed. I sat down on the blanket, my skirt, ankles, and shoes tinted, bright.

"After all the stinking pieces of paper he's put his name to. Documents that counted for nothing! The idiot. Your husband's an idiot, Gerda!"

"He's not my husband."

"Oh, he is. Very much your husband," muttered Rolf, standing before me. He was kneading his right arm with a calm, sure pressure. "I'm not sure whether he loves you or hates both of us, but whatever it is with him, the petition came back to Worshafter blank. An idiot! He must know it can't end there."

"He can't still love me," I whispered, horrified. "Not now, with everything." I clutched the mattress, as if it were tilting beneath me.

"Well, I'll find out. I'll send some good people to Passau." Rolf's face was stony. "No matter how this ends up, he isn't going to make people laugh that our child's a bastard."

"No." I seized his left hand, placed it on my stomach. "Our baby."

Slowly, he drew his hand away. "You don't understand, time is working against us. You can't stay here. You can't remain in Kreiswald." He walked over to the nightstand and jerked open the drawer. His strong wrists were bathed yellow in the light, the same yellow as my swollen ankles. He pushed the contents from one side to the other and, almost casually, as if to betray the tremor in his hands, withdrew a bulky brown envelope. He tossed it into my lap. "I know this sounds difficult, but at this point there's nothing more we can do. You'll have to do this, Gerda."

I didn't touch it. "What's in here?"

"Train ticket. Money. A good amount of money."

"You can't send me away! Not because of the baby. It can't come between us this way. It's not supposed to rob me of being with you."

"Gerda, there's a place outside of Trebic—"

"Czechoslovakia! You're sending me to the East! My brother Christoph died fighting in the East."

With a tight little smile, Rolf shook his head. "That was in Poland. This is entirely different, it's a kind of resort town, very quiet, really. I went there as a boy. I'll be able to visit you, you and the child."

"But you see," I heard myself explaining, "the baby's real job is to be inside me and make the two of us, you and me, into one. We're really your body now. Don't tell us to leave you, Rolf. You said it was safe here. You sent Torgood away so I could be with you. Is it true he wouldn't sign?"

"Gerda, you don't understand."

"Is that what you think?" I said in a high, choked voice. "I left my husband, I made up lies for the lawyer, and now I'm to get on some train? I understand more than you want to let me understand. Those silly guards—"

A siren wailed close by. There was a screech of brakes, maybe half a block away. *You! Jews—you halt!* someone shouted.

He said, "I want you to calm down."

"How can you send me away when we're at war!"

"We may be at war," he said grittily, "but we still live in society. You know what war is about? Theories of how people should live. And when the fighting's over, everyone will be branded by the choices they made. You can't offend society even in—most especially in—war." A trickle of sweat ran down his left temple. "Now, after a while, when the divorce is complete and the proper papers filed—when no one but some clerk will even see the timing and arrangement of things, then you can come back. You'll come back *right,* too, little one, trust me."

I could barely find my voice. "No one comes back from the East," I said.

"Don't talk nonsense. You'll be surprised by how comfortable the resort is." He turned. The back of his brown shirt was streaked with sweat, a line that like an x-ray brought out the secret of his spine. "I'm going to call for a car. It's best to go ahead and just do what we have to. At home, you can gather up a few things to take with you."

"No, Rolf, please."

From outside, a burst of gunfire. Someone began crying out in a desperate repetitive way: *Oh oh oh.* It was a painful sound, an ululation like a cat's. I was rigid, listening, then somehow I wasn't; I saw I was standing and the envelope had slid down my skirt and struck the floor.

Rolf's head twisted around. "What are you doing?" He walked back, picked it up.

"I'll do anything not to leave. You know I can't go. We have to be together until the end."

He laughed. "Listen to how fatalistic you are."

"Are you laughing at me?"

"Gerda, I told you that any separation is temporary."

"But why should I go? I know the official policy: Aryan men are to father as many children as possible, in wedlock or out. So, why should anyone say our child will be—"

"Stop fighting me!" He shoved the envelope against my breasts, forcing me against the nightstand. "You think I need to follow every little policy that comes down the road? I told you what I think: right now, it's his child and it's a bastard."

His fingers, five circles of pain, pressed down on my swollen breasts, even through the layers of money. His other hand hard in the small of my back. "Rolf, don't, you're hurting me. I can't keep my balance."

Fumbling, I pushed him off. The envelope stuck to his palm for a moment. Then its bottom seam came unglued. It emptied out, the brown rectangle fluttering down amid its unloosed contents.

With a groan, he got down on his knees. "Look at this mess," he said, and crawled over to pick up the furthest pieces first.

I didn't hesitate. I wrenched open the nightstand drawer, shoving my hands through the bits of paper, throat lozenges, string, pencils. Everything I grabbed on to was flimsy, light. Where was it? It was always right in the drawer. I wanted it.

Rolf looked up, his eyes wide as Prudmann's had been at seeing me suddenly in the station. "I thought you loved me," he said.

I wish I had shot him then as many times as I could. But even now, if the pistol had been there, I'm not sure I would have truly gone through with it, pulling a trigger against his dark head or his heart. Time clarifies nothing.

As I gazed down at him, bent over in front of me, I stopped shaking. "I do," I said. "Even after all this, I do. I will."

Slowly Rolf got to his feet, the reichsmarks springing out of his clasped hands like a bouquet. "Then we're agreed on our course of action?"

"We're agreed," I said. Outside, gunfire continued in spurts.

SECRET

7 September 1943

To Lt. Col. Dr. von Wedel
Army High Command . . .

From your letter of 26 ultimo I gathered that you are of the opinion that the firm of Krupp did not do its best to start the production of fuses at Auschwitz as soon as possible. I think there must be a misunderstanding . . . I can only say that a very close cooperation exists between this office and Auschwitz, and is assured also for the future.

With kind regards and Heil Hitler.

Yours faithfully

A. v. Bohlen[1]
[Alfried Krupp von Bohlen]

The Folktale

"THERE ONCE was a wife who complained to her husband that their house had become too small for them. The husband went to speak to the—what should I call him?—the *village wise man* about what he could do, short of depleting all his savings to expand the structure. The wise man told him to return home and lead his cow from the pasture into his house. Well, the husband did just that—he led the obedient cow right into the parlor, which was reserved for guests and always kept clean and neat. The wife was irate. 'Go back,' she said, 'and ask the wise man if that's what he really meant you to do.' The husband went back and the wise man said, 'Leave the cow where she is and bring in your pigs.' The husband brought in the pigs. 'Certainly you have misunderstood,' the wife cried as the pigs ran snorting for her larder. The husband insisted he hadn't, but the next morning, the wife in tears begged him to see the wise man again. 'Did you also bring in the chickens?' asked the wise man. So, that night the couple went to sleep with feathers flying about their heads and squawking and squabbling in their ears. The next morning they were awakened by the cock's brazen call and the cow's plaints to be milked. The wife tried to cook her husband's breakfast, but she couldn't rout the swine out of her kitchen. Of course the house smelled worse than a barn-yard, for it hadn't been constructed to contain animals who more naturally belonged outside its painted walls. Before the week was up, the couple realized their friends were avoiding them and they themselves were no longer speaking to each other—they were too busy clearing separate paths through the muck and disorder. Finally one day, someone knocked at their door. 'Take the cow, pigs, and chickens out,' said the wise man, by way of greeting. A few moments later, the couple looked about themselves, astonished. Why, how spacious their house was! How sweet!"

With a nervous grin, Felix slowly looked up from the book. "Well? What do you think?"

I held my breath. The air in the tiny front parlor seemed ready to burst, but then Willi, leaning back in his chair, his belly lifting like an overripe melon from atop his round thighs, broke into laughter. "Very good! In the East—ah, where I've been—you don't hear stories like that. It's about Lebensraum, isn't it? Very funny!"

"Yes, very good, Herr Breslauer," I enthused, nodding vigorously, as if at the story's cunning and not his own. "Just wonderful."

Felix almost slumped in relief. "Well!" he said again. Behind him, the early winter sun washed thinly across the window.

With his thumb, Willi pried a tear from the corner of his eye and wiped it along his workpants. The brown twill was none too clean from the three days he'd spent traveling. The trains were a mess; even parts of the tracks between Passau and Kreiswald had been bombed. "Tell me, Herr Breslauer," he said, "can I see that little book of yours? I'd like to send a copy to some friends I've left in the East. They're back there, still working on"—he shifted his weight—"a huge undertaking in terms of construction."

"I think your wife mentioned you were in the Polish Reich, Herr Hofflinger?"

"That's right—working hard outside a small hole of a town. One of those idiotic Polish names. Our government's renamed it, but it's all the same to me—just one big project. You wouldn't believe it all, Herr Breslauer, if I told you. Let me just say this, it's a kind of network of holding facilities the Reich wants built over there. My company's been in on the project from the start. Ah, a book like this would make my friends laugh at the end of a long day, right?"

Said Felix, "Sure. Excuse me for reaching across you, Frau Hofflinger; I want your husband to have this." And as he closed the slim blue book, Felix's eyes slid over toward me. A look I'm sure Willie didn't catch. Willi had always been a man who'd paid little attention to the details of romance. After the first year of our marriage I understood he'd as soon have his hands on a hammer as on a woman, but whichever he did have in his grip, he liked to use with a deft, deafening, repetitive force.

I pressed my shoulders back against the couch while Felix's arm extended across my chest. I could just catch the scent of my cologne on his wool sweater. Holding absolutely still, I watched the blue booklet pass from my lover's hand to my husband's.

"Thank you, Frau Hofflinger," Felix said, unnecessarily. He selected a sandwich from the platter I'd set before the three of us and took a bite.

"Give me a minute," muttered Willi, flipping open the book. He bent over the text. His red hair was coarse and thick; not at all the hair of a man in his fifties, the rusty fibers sprang from his square roundish head with unnerving strength.

Finally, reading, his attention was off me for the first time since his arrival. I tell you it all seemed unreal. Quite unexpectedly he had returned home from Poland; and maybe he'd felt the strangeness of this himself—because instead of using his key at his own front door, he'd knocked. I'd come in just ten minutes before. I'd spent the night across the street with Felix and was back in the kitchen, wiping off the plate I used for the cat's food. I didn't rush to answer the door; of course I thought it was probably a beggar. Or Felix, there was something he'd forgotten to tell me, and he'd come by on his way to his shop, was using the front door, as any tenant would. But unlike the other tenants, with a wide-brimmed hat shading his eyes and a mapmaker's flat leather portfolio pressed securely under his left arm, he was given to saluting me, properly and playfully. He claimed it was my face, shaped so like a heart, that he couldn't get enough of. For it alone, he said, he was my obedient slave. Only that morning he'd devoutly kissed my chin since I had denied him my lips, sucking them back between my teeth like the crone I would one day become—and much sooner than he, fourteen years my junior. Felix had hardly flinched, though he usually was fastidious about matters of the body.

I put the cat's refilled plate down on the linoleum, then I went to answer the door. "Willi!" I gave the sash on my robe a tighter tug.

"Surprise," he exhaled a tobacco-tinged breath, "it *is* me, come here." Eagerly, his nose darted through my hair. "*Ahh,*" he inhaled deeply. He brought his cold, stubbly face to mine and opened his mouth. With the next breath, we were kissing—and it was so familiar and strange! There was a sore inside his right cheek. His tongue kept pushing mine against its cratered surface. A wet, bloodless-blood taste. "So,

Erika"—he pulled back and laughed—"I'm back for good."
From outside on the street came the winding mewl of the
cat demanding to be let in for its meal.

Angrily I wiggled away. "You might have written to tell
me when you were coming!"

He crouched down and, with a full swing of his arm,
shoved in a suitcase, the metal buckles scraping and squeal-
ing across the floorboards. "You know I'm no writer." He
looked up with his head just below my breasts and added,
grinning, "Besides, a wife should expect her husband at any
time."

"Oh, Willie, you've been gone more than three years! I
would have gone crazy, always expecting you. And now,
'forty-two is nearly over, too. You have no idea what it's been
like." As the tears squeezed in confusion out of my eyes, I
thought how I had to get to Felix and warn him not to come
for lunch as he usually did: *My husband has returned, it's
over! Don't take it to heart. Goodbye!*

But all morning, he kept me busy. He asked for breakfast
along with the rental account books; asked me to unpack and
sort through his clothes; then, since full baths were no longer
allowed except on Saturdays, asked if I would warm up the
kettle. Sponge baths were allowed since they didn't use as
much heating fuel.

With the basin steaming in my hands, I climbed the stairs
to the bedroom. Willi was sitting before the window on the
short wooden stool, his back to me. "When did the worker
transports start coming into Kreiswald?" he asked, gazing
down at the street.

I set the bowl on the washstand. Over the rumble of traffic
on Ludwigstrasse, I said, "To tell you the truth, I haven't
seen any."

"Really?" His head swiveled. "These are the first? No
other Russians or worse Slavic types have been sent in from

the occupied territories? That's astounding. Are you sure?"

"I don't know, Willi. Maybe I've seen some."

I glanced at the bed; if the covers were dusty, he'd see they hadn't been slept in for two nights. I stepped in front, blocking his view. "It's been a hard time and you know how I can be. I can't tell you whether it's the first, third, or thirtieth."

"Well, keep your eyes open. I've used transports, you know, at Auschwitz." He paused and rubbed his chin. "You know, on the project. The construction. It's just a big camp, Erika. Anyway, they're called animal-men. Work just like mules." Again, he turned to the window. "I wonder who's getting this allotment shipped in? The town needs to set them to work repairing the train tracks and drainage ditches and such. Wash me, Erika, will you?" He peeled off his sweater; the undershirt, clinging inside-out, came with it.

I caught my breath. Over his back seemed to be pasted one of Felix's detailed topographical maps—but unlike my sweet Felix's work, what I saw was just filth, just a yellow, sour expanse of skin. Brown hairs pressed stiffly against the scabs, insect bites, pus-filled pimples and the long, raised, pinkish trails where he had scratched at himself. He certainly hadn't left Kreiswald looking like this. I never could have borne it. Mechanically, I picked up the dishtowel, a prettily embroidered square of cotton I'd taken from the rental flat the same day Felix moved into it. Wetting it, I wiped between the shoulder blades.

"Don't be so delicate. Come on, rub me, bear down."

I closed my eyes and leaned into him. This wrecked back was my husband's.

"Better!" Willi sighed. He slumped forward, his spine barely protruding under the thick layer of skin.

Surprisingly, the warmth of the water and the way his flesh began to pinken and shine was soothing. That he had so much weight on him, too, was exotic; no one else could get quite enough to eat anymore, not with rationing. I scrubbed harder. Another twist of the towel and in the basin the soapy gray scum thickened on the water's surface. With a little thrill, I began to wonder just how much dead skin I could skim off of him. He might continue to melt down under my touch, like rendered fat. I rolled the cloth down the left side of his rib cage, then down the right. My movements became more and more languid.

"Who's that?" he murmured sleepily.

Suddenly I heard it, the front doorbell was ringing. My head jerked up. "No one," I said. "A beggar. Willi, they always come at lunch time, it's too pitiful, with their stories about what they lost in the air raids. I can't bear listening to one more! Be quiet; maybe he'll go away."

But, of course, the brass knocker now began to thud against the door. Willie grabbed his undershirt and wiped it over his back. He got to his feet. "It's time to show my face around here again."

A moment later, his voice rumbled up the stairs, "Erika, a tenant."

"Introduce yourself!" I tried to keep the panic out of my tone. Hurriedly I shook off my hands.

With a grunt, Willi looked up from the little book in his lap. "Herr Breslauer, why did you tell me that you stopped by to show this pamphlet to my wife?"

Felix stopped chewing. Above his head, the blackout shade fluttered; in the last air raid, a crack had opened at the top of the wooden frame and allowed in drafts. "I stopped by," said Felix slowly, "because Frau Hofflinger mentioned to me the other week, when I was paying my rent, that she would enjoy reading something light. I came by to drop this off. I certainly didn't expect to be asked in to share your midday meal, you're too kind." He barely glanced at me. I thought the lie came off well.

"You wanted her to read this?" Willie held up the pamphlet.

"Why do you question it?"

Willi said, "A Jew book shouldn't be brought into a decent home. Look at this word: *rabbi.* Not *village wise man,* as you'd read aloud. There are rabbis in all the stories!"

"Well, it's that," said Felix, shaking his head with a little laugh, his narrow face as red now as Willi's fleshy one, "and also not that." He straightened the cuff on his shirt so just a touch of white showed under the sweater.

"Not what?" Willi stared.

"Not, as you say, a Jew book." Felix settled in against the cushions. He seemed about to put his arm atop the back of the couch until he realized he would also, then, be embracing me. "Premier Printers," he said, leaning forward, "did once belong to a Hebrew. But about a year ago, he must have been sent east to work for the State. Since he hadn't sold beforehand, the government had to put the shop up for auction. I won the bid—it included all the contents. Along with the major inventory, there were, oh, ten or twelve of these booklets. They were hidden in the back storeroom under some papers. Obviously a small project that hadn't been completed. At the time, I didn't bother myself with them. Yesterday, I picked one up. Immediately I saw why Volkmann had taken on the work. You saw it, too."

Willi shifted his weight in the chair. "Well, it was funny, I'll give you that."

Felix smiled nervously. Wedged between his front teeth was a crumb of dark pumpernickel from the sandwich. My heart twisted; he would be mortified when he realized he'd been talking with it there.

"My feeling, Herr Hofflinger," he continued, "is that some

things in this life just get off to the wrong start. Make a few modifications here and there—in the characters' names and in the locations and such—and this becomes an Aryan book. *Tales of Our Countrymen,* I thought to call it. One thousand—and more!—fresh copies bound and pasted of *Tales of Our Countrymen* against a dozen folded proofs of *Stories from Rivah.* With this, I can branch out from maps, start a new sideline. So you see, it is quite simple: Frau Hofflinger, your wife and my landlady, actually was the opportunity to try my ideas out."

"She was your experiment. You wanted her to like it."

Felix glanced at me. "Sure—like it, of course, to an extent. I think the full reaction is the one you've given me. How glad I am, Herr Hofflinger, that you were here!"

"I see," said Willi slowly, chewing on the inside of his right cheek.

Felix flushed. "I have an appointment tomorrow with someone in government, an official who's especially interested in just this kind of thing. I need to secure certain approvals, since paper's rationed these days for most other publishing projects. As successful as my mapmaking line is, there's also a market for something light, like this."

Willi nodded again. With a little jolt, I realized that my tongue tingled. I could taste what he was secretly tasting, that sore.

"I think it's quite possible to accomplish what I'm proposing, Herr Hofflinger. I think that what happened here, in this room, proves my point—that is, that this little book has potential. It makes people laugh."

Both their faces were strained as if the effort involved in making and following the argument were physical. The air, in fact, smelled of sweat. I glanced at Felix—with his head pulled back on his neck so that his Adam's apple protruded like a defensive rooster's—and again back at Willi, but so close were the three of us that I couldn't gaze at one without some hand or knee of the other thrust in the way. I felt a sudden excitement: both men wanted me.

Lurching forward over his stomach, Willi slapped the book down on the table. "Finish that lousy meatless sandwich, Herr Breslauer," he roared. "And put me down for a half-dozen books from your first printing. I want them free, too. If you're getting new machinery, then you'll probably need some construction work done. Fine! I'm your man."

Felix sat back, stunned. "You want a job?"

"Willi"—I turned on the couch—"your first afternoon home! Do you really mean to work with Herr Breslauer?"

He stood to stretch, his massive arms winding over his head, the fingers curled. "Why not," he yawned. "I have good contacts from my last project. It makes sense to keep them fresh. Let's have a look at this shop you own, Herr Breslauer."

Felix rose all at once. "I'm eager for you to see it. Maybe you can offer me some suggestions on the structure itself, on how to make use of the space more efficiently. I was thinking I'd have to expand, but only if I don't have to tear down too many walls, risk all that dust and disorder, not to mention the expense—"

"I'm coming, too!" I got to my feet.

Both of them turned. "Why, Erika," said Willi gently, as if to a child, "I won't disappear again. I'm home for good, I promise." He reached into his back pocket and, pulling out a crumpled handkerchief, noisily blew his nose. "Still bloody," he muttered, glancing down at the flecked mucus. "Do we have any salve in the house? This sore I've got won't heal on its own."

I hesitated.

Felix opened his mouth to speak but then simply shut it. He bent for his portfolio.

Hastily I said, "I'll have to buy some at the pharmacy."

Willi daubed the underneath of his nose. "Then get your coat and come with us. I'll be right back." With an apologetic shrug, he patted the handkerchief into his back pocket and said to Felix, "You know what travel does to a body."

As soon as the door to the W.C. shut and his flatulence was at least muffled, Felix and I hugged. After Willi, Felix's bones felt hard, unprotected. My left cheek pressed up against his sweater; the fibers smelled of me. I wanted to rub more of my scent off on them. I was wearing the perfume he'd bought me from a friend stationed in France.

"We did it, we fooled him," he breathed, nipping at my neck.

"He can't find out. Not ever."

"This is crazy. It's impossible."

"But you're going ahead, having him work for you. Aren't you?"

He straightened, his whole body thinking of an answer. "No, I won't, not unless some profit's in it."

"Well," I whispered, and tweaked his nose, "you've become such a prudent burgher."

His eyes flicked down the hall toward the toilet. "Have you let him touch you?"

My face flushed. I gave a little laugh. "It's clear he's come home."

"This is all impossible," he repeated. Sharply then: "Get your fur. He's pulled the chain on the toilet."

I elbowed past him and was arranging the black tiny paws on my fox wrap so the legs crossed where the first joint would have been when Willi ambled down the hall and into the foyer. "Ready," I said brightly.

Said Willi, "I can pick up the tube of salve on my way, Erika."

"But I'll do it!"

"No need," he said curtly, and pulled his coat off the hanger. "What street is your shop on, Herr Breslauer?"

Felix smiled. In the confusion, I hadn't told him about the dark spongy bit caught in his teeth. Now it was too late; pointing it out would seem to Willi too intimate a gesture for a relationship based only on business. Still grinning, Felix said, "You see, Herr Hofflinger, like your hard-to-pronounce Polish town, this street was another one of those things that got the wrong start in life." He tucked his portfolio under his right arm. "Now it's called Sommerstrasse. All four blocks have been renovated. As a builder, you're sure to appreciate the changes. The government put some money into it. It gives people heart, something to look at, instead of the unfortunate destruction that often comes with war."

"The street's very popular," I put in quickly. "I like strolling along it even when I have no chores to do."

Willi leaned over and kissed my cheek, the one burnished by Felix's sweater. "Stop worrying about me. I can get some salve without any trouble. I know my way around Kreiswald, remember? Let's go, Herr Breslauer. A man like me doesn't like to be out of work for too long." He turned the doorknob. With a wretched meow, in shot the cat. Its head low, it wound frantically between our legs. I'd forgotten all about the poor little beast.

I grabbed Willi's outstretched arm. "Don't! It's my pet, it's all right."

He turned an astonished face. "You've named that animal?"

"Just *cat*. I was lonely, I told you I needed company."

The white hairs of its scarred, ropey tail disappeared around the door to the kitchen. "Erika," Willi sighed as if he'd glimpsed what my life had been like while he was away.

"It's gotten used to coming inside during the day. That's all. It stays out at night."

"Thank you again, Frau Hofflinger," said Felix, clearing his throat.

"No, not at all," I said, over the greedy scraping sounds of a plate being nosed across the linoleum.

The moment the door clicked shut, I didn't stop to take off my fur but ran up the stairs and over to the bedroom window. Directly below me stood Willi and Felix. An open-backed truck passed them—empty except for one of those foreign laborers in the back gripping onto the guard rail; then they stepped off the curb and into the wind. From this angle each looked to be stepping down onto his own shadow's chest. Their strides were different, of course. But as I watched them cross the cold, snowless street, I saw that neither would allow the other to get so much as a half-meter in front of him. They were competing.

Giggling, I tossed the spread off the pillows and fell stomach first upon the bed. "Darling!" I whispered, "oh, my darling—too." I rolled partway onto my left side, then back again onto my right. I was the mistress of two beds, wasn't I? Closing my eyes, I kissed the fleshy web of my hand, between thumb and index finger. "My darling pets!" That I could have only one at a time made the other—the one temporarily locked out of my room—even more exciting. I kissed my hand again, rolling back and forth until the wrinkles in the sheets were no longer days old but fresh. Behind my eyelids red circles floated. A woman called out from somewhere outside: *Ernst, hurry up, go to the right! I can't be late.* I thought about the key to Felix's flat, about Willi's voracious first embrace. Then I saw myself taking that half-wishbone of a key from the desk drawer and in the next moment slipping it against Willi's bristling chest. I rubbed my hand across the fox's muzzle and back against the grain of its back fur. I kept going back and forth. The air popped with static.

* * *

For the next few days I blushed like a girl of fifteen, feeling alternately guilty and joyous about the electricity I made crackle around me. As for Willi and Felix, they were as excited as boys with a secret. Underneath the old surfaces, our new lives were getting ready to burst out. It was thrilling, yes, but also exhausting, to keep everything from exploding to pieces.

And so, oddly, almost adolescently, we began a period of being chaste. That very first night, Willi came home and brought one bottle of Riesling, a second one of schnapps—and Felix. By the time it was curfew, the bottles were empty. Pushing back the kitchen chair and pulling me up, Willi reached for Felix, wrapping him under his other arm, as much to steady himself as anything else. "To the beginning," he announced, swaying—and swaying us, our one shadow sliding between the wall and the blackout blind—"of a great venture."

"To the total expansion of my business."

"Better—to its success." To me, Willie stage-whispered, "Tomorrow he meets with his government official, that's for special permits, and then with Helmut Frasier, you know, for a bank loan."

"We'll have workers in no time; Willi promised to get them." And in a light, happy voice, Felix continued explaining (as if earlier I hadn't heard!): This wall moved back, that one torn down, a partition built dividing the shop. Everything in its place—Willie and he had agreed. They would keep what was working *working*—unaffected by what was to be built. So, anything to do with mapmaking—the inkbaths and screens and such—would stay where it was, but everything else would be planned for behind the partition, in the back. There'd be no mixing of the two processes. Printing books was a new venture for the firm and every last detail had to be handled in good order, on time, and without confusion. Willi was adamant about that, said Felix, swaying. His fingers tickled my back (behind Willi's back). He said, again: Willi was adamant that the shop's big machinery be kept out of sight of the customers. As such, a new wall would go up, that is, something thicker than the flimsy half-wall Volkmann had worked behind. Willi, he said, was adamant about changing the reception area into a room as simple and bright as the waiting room of a station. And he himself had agreed.

"Enough, Herr Breslauer!" With a giggle, I pulled away.

They'd also agreed, I learned, that I wasn't to come by until they said so. But just as the cat brought me its trophies of dead mice, so my most darling pets brought me their stories of how the project—Willi had been sent a transport of eight foreign workers—was going. My job was to listen to these stories and gobble them up. In truth I didn't need to listen, because as soon as they walked through the door, I could sniff out how the day had gone.

For a time, all this—the stories and kitchen table camaraderie—was satisfaction enough. But as the weeks went by, I became restless. In the middle of housecleaning, I'd find myself suddenly rooting through the drawers for an extra key to Felix's flat or I'd realize while listening to Frieda Worshafter fret as we both waited in line at the butcher's for whatever stringy cuts of meat our ration coupons might bring, that my tongue was poking at the inside of my cheek. Then it began that sitting between Willi and Felix in my front parlor, I felt I was being smothered—all because neither so much as laid his hand on me! In the midst of what should have been plenty, I was wasting away.

From the stuffed chair, Willi continued the story. The drainage ditch by the north wall was done. It had taken three days—each night the earth froze another half-meter down—

but the sewage pipes were in and covered. Luckily, there'd been no snow for some time; the ground was bare, which helped move things along.

"He's still on schedule," said Felix, not looking up from the accounts ledger balanced on his knee. He and I were sharing the couch. In my lap was a squall of black socks. For the second time, I aimed the damp ends of the threads through the darning needle.

Willi said, "But now I have dysentery running through four of the workers, those mules from Silesia." He gulped in some air and launched into another story. They weren't working hard enough. And the stink from dysentery, besides. He decided to order one of the healthy workers over to the pump to fill up the buckets—a technique he was borrowing from the commanders on his last project. Then whenever the Silesian mules sat down, he had someone throw a bucket of water over them. And that water was cold, too. Like ice. They'd jump up. Two birds with one stone— faster work, to keep warm, and less filth. Once this project was done, then they could rest. You had to be stern with them, they didn't understand any language.

Shuddering, I pulled the wool through the eye. Willi's conversation had become much like his snoring: a terrible, incomprensible first burst, then numbing repetition. It was better not to listen. Working my left hand through a sock, I concentrated instead on weaving the patch to close up the toe-hole. At the end, I bit off the excess strings. Happily, there was enough left dangling from the needle; I wouldn't have to rethread.

"She is good," Felix said smoothly, "thank you." The pages of his ledger flapped, or maybe it was the blackout blind.

Said Willi, "Every time I come in, she jumps up and brings me a big mug of ersatz coffee. That steam in my face— wonderful."

Felix smiled. "Just what I told her to do."

I waited for a police siren to get fainter. "Who are you talking about?"

"Why, Felix's new assistant. Thea Wenngarten. Is it Thea Wenngarten or Wenngartens, Felix?"

I stuck the needle into the couch cushion between us.

"Thea Wenngarten." Felix kicked the cat away from rubbing against his pantslegs. "There's no *s.*"

"Someone new?" I turned. "Tell! When did you hire her? Is she very smart and pretty? Tell me everything."

Felix leaned over and began to pick the white and brown hairs off his pants. "Five weeks ago Heinrich Maser's reserve unit was called up—sure, didn't I say something?—so I had to replace him. I thought I should try a girl, instead. That is, it made no sense to hire another man of draftable age." He paused. The skin at the back of his neck, above his collar, was slowly turning red. "I think I'm probably safe, but since the trouble on the Russian front, they've been drafting men up to fifty. The communists don't know enough to give in."

"Sorry." Willi shifted in his chair. He'd never gotten rid of his gassiness. "Myself, I saw fifty a few years ago."

I slid my hand into the next sock and spread the material. Three holes opened up, one not that small. "And Fräulein Wenngarten? Is she going to stay long, do you think?"

Felix bent over, his face hidden from me, on the other side of his knees. Jointed like a spider's legs, his fingers were feeling their way down the crease of his pants. One white cat hair floated above his knuckles. "I need an assistant," he mumbled to the floor, "and she wants to learn. Fräulein Wenngarten is, well, she's very good at the business."

Willi snorted. "You think she's good at more than that." Arms hanging off the chair, he was waving the bad air behind him. "You stop it," he snarled; the cat had slunk up and was batting at his left hand. "No playing, you just keep away."

Felix said, alarmed, "Playing? Willi—*what?* What? I haven't touched Thea yet." He swirled dizzyingly upward to a sitting position and from the slanting cushion between us the needle popped right out.

So he wanted her, this young, willing milk cow! Oh, how greedy he was, and I hadn't caught it. And I was available, I was close by, I was right here.

I was still wearing the sock on my hand. Leaning down, I swung that arm as wide as I could: with a yowl, the cat skidded around on its back, into the end table. I said, "I want to go to bed. Let's not wait to get too tired, Willi, all right?" Then I seized his hand and squeezed it inside my black paw.

Felix was shaking his long head from side to side, trying to clear it so he could hear more than his surging blood. He looked ridiculous, so red in the face. What an ass.

In the past I'd always kept my eyes closed. Now I was no longer used to his lurching rhythms but to Felix's more predictable, almost passive gliding and I needed to see where he was. Where was he going next? Suddenly, with a quick push upward, Willi drew close to my face. It was dark. The bureau mirror gleamed like mercury through the bristles of his hair.

"All right?" He panted, wide-eyed.

"Thank god we're done with that stage we were stuck at."

His face dripped onto mine. "I'm back all the way now, Erika, believe me."

I kissed him. My tongue darting in, I could taste it, still there—that shocking new tinge of pleasure. "Good."

With a growl, he started again. This time, I couldn't seem to hold on to him; he was everywhere at once: cajoling me with the hairs on his chest, with the oxenlike fall of his belly, the pads of flesh at his hips, his hard, immovable, straining legs. "Erika, no one like you, not where I was. Slower, come up with your hips, ah. Ah. The women were nothing to look at, just good bones. You know, where I was—" He kissed my neck, he kissed me between my breasts. "I didn't touch them. I wouldn't betray you. They were everywhere but they were dead to me. All right, move up, again. Good place. I didn't look at any of them." He licked my stomach, slowly circled my navel. "I brushed them away—flies. You know? You know, where I was."

I nodded, gasping. "Poland, the project."

He ran his tongue up my left side, over my ribs. A wet path of fire. "Thousands were there."

"You mean female laborers, Willi?"

"Undesirables—all different kinds. Young. Not so young. They were all over. Believe me? I never betrayed you?"

"Yes. Yes."

He moved my hand. "Here, help me now."

Glimpsed through the doorway, we would have made a curious sight; for a moment I seemed to be standing there, watching how everything happened—then I was sprawled back on the bed. The mattress felt too small for our arms and legs. My body slid underneath his, my head suspended part-way over the edge, into the air. Our two bodies lifting and grinding. A surge. I threw my arms across his blistered back.

I should have gone right to sleep, but I couldn't. Each time I was about to drift away on the deep rumbling river of Willi's snoring, something featherish lit on me. Just the small-est point on my neck, or cheek or left heel would twitch me awake. That gnat was Felix. Felix and his cow Thea! I wanted my joy tonight to be his punishment and I would have slept well enough if I could have been sure that his own imagina-tion—of my having sex with Willi—was making him restless.

But lying under a mound of blankets and pressed up against Willi's back, I couldn't be sure.

At five, naked, I crept out of bed. I didn't have my night-gown, but I didn't dare turn on a light—and not because of the curfew. Midway on the landing, I paused, arms over my breasts. From upstairs came the slow guttural outbursts, apparently undisturbed. I hurried, my feet cold on the bare floor.

As soon as I reached the bottom, the windowpanes began rattling; trucks—large and from the vibrations, fully weighted—were going past. Holding my breath, I crept to the hall window. I had to wait while seven passed. They were loaded with people. In the starry night, I saw blurred faces and, flapping back and forth below these, the yellow blinking of six-pointed stars. Hands waving: the glint of a ring, or fingernail. Jews, not laborers.

The minute seemed unbearably long until the last truck made the right turn onto Osterstrasse. After a while the rumbling got fainter. Then the street was still.

In the dark, I picked up the phone. I walked as far as the cord would allow. Facing the empty parlor, tethered, I shivered through two rings, three . . . six.

"Hello," he said in a lash of static.

As if struck, my head jerked up.

"Hello?" he repeated, his voice strange, tight. "Yes? Who is it?"

Sweating, I strained forward from my shoulders.

"Who is it? Hello?"

I bit my tongue. From high in my throat came a whining sound, a begging sound like a dog makes.

"Is it—?" he faltered. "Is it you?"

I pressed a hand between my legs. My whimpering got louder. The sound was squeezed together, all vowels.

He started to whisper wild, incomprehensible things.

Maybe one of them was my name, I don't know. Whatever he was saying, whatever words he was using, didn't seem to mean anything. Finally, he began to whine back.

With his foot and still seated, Willi shoved a chair out from the table. "Door's open," he shouted, "I'm busy."

Sniffing, Felix walked back into the kitchen. "What are you having? It's late."

Willi sopped up the red gravy on the back of his fork. "Erika got some extra sausage with her coupons, don't ask me how. Want one?"

"Sure. I have an appetite today. Must be the weather—the air's very mild, I think we're having a thaw." He took the chair. "Good morning, Erika."

Said Willi, picking a bit of gristle off his tongue, "Might as well call him by his first name, Erika, he started it."

The wienerwurst, sizzling, fat as a puppy's tail, rolled to the edge of the plate as I set it before him. "Good morning," I hesitated, "Felix."

He stuck his fork into the casing and a jet of yellow oil spurted out sideways. "Well, thank you, Erika." The two of them looked at each other, rolled their eyes, and laughed. I laughed, too. Then I sat between them to finish my plate of sliced sausage. Two pink circles, blind meaty eyes, stared back at me. How good they tasted, a special treat—juicy and loud as I chewed! That something solid held this much moisture was wonderful.

"About what's next," said Willi, knife scraping across the plate, "the new press is installed in the back. You're going ahead with the dry run, right?"

Felix's narrow cheeks bulged. He nodded.

"Then I'll have the debris loaded up and out, first thing. It'll be gone in an hour, hour and a half. I can lend you my laborers after that, if you want. Let's see if they can do something new. I'll put them back to work for me after you run your test. I can use them until the fifteenth of the month. More than enough time to finish up."

"Good." Felix swallowed. "Fräulein Wenngarten made certain that the dumping permit is in order, so you won't have any problem there. I think," he said, swallowing again, "I might have to let her go. I'm considering it."

I stopped chewing. He wasn't saying this to Willi, but to me. Her possible dismissal—it had to be my gift for last night.

With a grunt, Willi pushed back from the table. "Let's go ourselves."

"Sure. One more bite."

"For your little pet, Erika." Squatting, Willi put his greasy plate down on the floor. "Home by dark, I hope."

Mouth full, I tried to keep my lips together, but they split apart in a grin. I turned my happy face from one to the other. So, I was enough for both of them!

"Thanks for the meal, Erika," said Felix, and he put his plate on the linoleum, too.

And there the dishes stayed, the circles of grease congealing on them. I cleaned the rest of the kitchen, dusted and straightened up the front parlor. Finally, I heard a scratching at the front door. But instead of the cat scooting in between my ankles, there—with the stillness of a life-sized statue, stood a beggar.

"Please, gnädige Frau," she said, and held out her hand.

I glanced only once at the grimy face. She had on a shawl that had once been white but was now matted with dirt. "Oh," I said, "well, I was looking for my cat."

The shawl slipped down to her shoulders. "I can find it for you." Eagerly she twisted her filthy neck around.

I shook my head. "No, it's probably somewhere nearby."

"But what does it look like? Please tell me."

I stepped back into the house, though the air was mild.

"Let me find your sweet pet for you, gnädige Frau." Putting two fingers to her mouth, she gave a piercing whistle.

"Stop it!" I looked down at the newspaper in my hand. If I gave her the *Kompass* and she managed to sell it before suppertime when the new edition came out, she could make a few pfennigs. "Here. Just take this."

The air thudded, a single soft explosion, like snow falling all at once off some roof. "God in heaven," she whispered, her eyes widening. Grabbing the paper, she ran to the curb and looked up.

"What's wrong?" I said. "What is it?"

Then it happened. Above the line of Ludwigstrasse's chimneys the jigsaw piece of our sky was still blue and unscratched: there wasn't even a trail of a cloud running through it, not a wisp from a plane: it wasn't even an instant. I tell you the air raid sirens opened up. In a single burst, the church bells began tolling. I ran to the curb but the beggar pushed past me. She fled to the center of the street, which looked like it was tilting with the great cathedral bells. On it, cars and trucks were scattered, each one pointing in a different direction. Drivers and passengers headed for the pavement. There, others were trying to hurry, but it was as if they were fighting up an incline. My neighbors poured out of their doorways. With a cry, I spun about. My house was safer than any public shelter. My front door was still open; I ran to it; I put my palms against the front panel, to push it, and the wood trembled just like rain. Inside, the sound of glass breaking. From the parlor, uncaged, the air raid sirens careening in midshriek.

Somehow what was happening couldn't be true. I closed my eyes. How far was it? How far was the shop?

I ran down Ludwigstrasse, my arms pushing out to either side between the rippling buildings. The growl of the British squadron flew after me.

* * *

"Let me in! Open up!" Again, I reached through the iron grillwork and pounded on the plate glass window. Why hadn't it broken? Behind it, like a stage set, stood Premier Printers' newly constructed waiting area. It had the freshly painted white walls they'd told me about. Framed maps hung on the walls at one-meter intervals; the hands on the round clock read noon, exactly. I had no idea if that was the correct time; where I stood each second exploded. I shuddered. Everything in there was too normal. The room didn't seem real. But if only I could get inside anyway! If only I could be *any*where but out here! I pressed closer; in the open archway behind the counter something seemed to be moving. Something was alive in the back room, behind the white wall. Squinting, I saw a black metal rod working deftly as a thresher; its shadow fell forward, under it. And working in opposition to it—leaning back, coming forward again— was that an arm in a cast? "Please," I shouted, "help me! The police station's been destroyed. It's burning. Willi, do you hear me? Felix!"

Another explosion to the west. I put my hands over my ears, not from the noise—awful enough—but the air pressure. Back against the wall, I slid to the ground. *Kristina, where are you?* some man called over and over. *Answer me, Kristina.* Sickened, coughing from the soot thrown up by the fires started from phosphorous bombs, I lurched into the alley. I fell over lengths of drainage pipes, over hods of red bricks. It was easier to crawl.

On all fours, I rounded the corner. I couldn't believe what I saw next—the back wall was only three-quarters finished. All that closed off the entry was a canvas tarp—and it was held down by nothing more than a length of rope. There was no other barrier. Shaking, I stood up and slipped the knot. The canvas flapped over my head in a wide, dirtied wing.

With one step, the feeling of being safe overwhelmed me. I quickly tied the tarp back in place. Outside the bombs fell erratically; here the clatter and roar of the machinery was loud and repetitive and precisely regulated. In the dim light—bare bulbs swinging from wires looped over the ceiling beams—the shadows of the workers' heads and hands spread across the dark shapeless machines or sank between them for the briefest of moments. There wasn't a meter of unused space anywhere. It was filled right to the walls.

Everything was moving almost at double time. I couldn't believe how fast the foreign laborers worked. One, his striped uniform spattered with mud, kept screaming something in some language at two workers loading a cart. His hand chopped at the air. But their hands moved even faster. The taller one stopped shouting; they took up their places. Leaning in with their weight, they pushed the cart right past me as if I weren't there, so hard were they concentrating on not spilling the awkward piles of paper atop it.

Of course, I'd forgotten: this was the dry run. They were about to feed the first of these skin-white sheets into their new presses. My two men—nothing could stop them! This was the real beginning of *Tales of Our Countrymen*. This was the test that should show how, after all the plans and troubles, they were staring, finally, at their success.

Out of the roaring, Willie barked my name. Felix was right behind at his heels.

Laughing, neighing, I ran toward them, weaving between the throbbing machinery, the racing, sweating workers. I was going to tell them that if we had to, we should just move in here; we would do fine. The three of us. I knew for sure, deep in my bones, that no enemy bomb would ever touch this place. If it had lasted through this attack, then it surely would endure until the end of this wretched war.

Der Chef
des SS-Wirtschafts-Verwaltungshauptamtes
A II/3 Reinl./Mo/Ro Geh.Tgb. . 61/44

Berlin, den 4.7.44

Geheim

732/4

Betr.: Uhrenverteilung.

An den
Reichsführer-SS
SW 11
Prinz-Albrecht-Str. 8

Reichsführer!

Bei der Amtsgruppe D in Oranienburg befinden sich 3000 instandgesetzte Wecker und kleine Tischuhren.

Die Amtsgruppe D hat mitgeteilt, daß innerhalb der Konzentrationslager für die Ausstattung der Wachstuben etwa 500 Wecker hiervon benötigt werden.

Ich bitte die Verteilung wie folgt zu genehmigen:

500 Uhren an die Amtsgruppe D,
zur Verteilung an die Konzentrationslager für Wachstuben
2500 Uhren an den Gauleiter von Berlin, Reichsminister
Dr. Goebbels,
zur Verteilung über die NSV. an bombengeschädigte Berliner.

Pohl

SS-Obergruppenführer und
General der Waffen-SS

The Chief of the
SS-Wirtschaftsverwaltungshauptamt
A II/3 Reinh./Mo./Ro. Geh. Tgb. Nr. 61/44

Berlin, July 4, 1944
SECRET

Re: Distribution of clocks

To the Reichsführer SS
Berlin SW 11
Prinz Albrechtstr. 8

Reichsführer!

The Amtsgruppe D in Oranienburg has 3000 repaired alarm clocks and other small table clocks.

The Amtsgruppe D has informed us that it requires approx. 500 of the alarm clocks for the concentration camp guard rooms. I request permission to distribute the clocks as follows: 500 clocks for the Amtsgruppe D, for concentration camp guard rooms. 2500 clocks for the Berlin Gauleiter, Dr. Goebbels, for distribution through the NSV to Berlin citizens who have been bombed out.

signed: Pohl
SS-Obergruppenführer
General der Waffen-SS

The Shift

THE POLICE STATION was burning. The front door, blown straight off its hinges, lay almost unscratched on the far side of the street. Pinned under it was a cat. Or that's what it seemed, given the length of the tail, the only part of the animal sticking out. In situations that threaten to overwhelm, keep your eye on the small detail. That's my motto. That's how to get yourself through a disaster.

Even in the mayhem, people wouldn't walk across the door. So it was salvageable, and maybe after the engineers had their say, the outer walls would be, also. Most of the roof was gone; it had received at least one direct hit. The upper floors were in flames. I was still bleary-eyed from only three hours' sleep. My shift had ended at 6:45 that morning when, as always, Rolf Terskan had taken over. When I'd walked out of the station—when it was still whole—I could feel an unseasonable mildness in the air; *this* after a bitter snowless stretch. The first day in February. The sun was just coming up. First it poked out from one after another of the side alleys, then on Danubestrasse it floated—a firm pale yolk on the choppy waves of the river. I was a man whose eyes were shut from just after dawn until midafternoon, but I still noticed the sun. It's what the moon is to you—it's what points me toward bed.

I didn't want my life to be any different. Working in darkness is simple. Few new ideas and even fewer activities first take shape in the dark, despite what most people—all of them dreamers!—believe. The night schedule is set by what happens in tumult during the day. Since I got the rank of commander back in '36, seven years before, I chose the second shift. I wanted to take my ease along with my work. But in times of crisis, like anyone else, I wasn't given a choice.

I was in bed when the British planes set their noses toward Kreiswald. Later, once they'd finished their business and the all-clear sounded, I climbed from my cellar back to the world. Horrifying things. Off-kilter. It was noon. In full daylight, the station was burning. The air was so vile I had to hold a wet towel over my nose and mouth. My eyes wouldn't stop tearing.

"You, Eikenhorn," I shouted at the first policeman I saw stumbling through the layers of smoke, "where are you taking that file?"

"Orders—" he panted, lugging the grey metal cabinet across the street, "from Commander Terskan." Tall and thin, he looked almost comical with his arms and legs bent like pipe cleaners against the weight of the file cabinet.

I spoke over the wailing of the sirens. "Well, help me now. I need you to lift this door. We can use it again, yes?" Tossing away the towel, I began to unbutton my uniform jacket so I could bend down. I had too much of a paunch to work with the jacket closed.

"I'm to save the files, Commander Gruber. Commander Terskan said I'm not to stop." He continued moving forward.

"I'm to put the records in whatever houses nearby are still standing."

"That's insane, hold on a minute. You can't take this into a civilian house."

He clutched the cabinet. "My orders are I'm not to stop. We just finished moving out your desk, the one the two of you use. He said to save that first. Kremmetz," he shouted, coughing, "come quickly. The night commander needs help." But in the roar of flames and timber, Kremmetz, carrying off two of the evidence crates, didn't hear.

Said Eikenhorn, almost pleading, "I'm not to stop, Commander Gruber." He swayed, even with his feet planted apart. He couldn't bear up much longer, I could see; it was either keep moving or fall.

But it made no sense. The information in our police files was classified. With despair I watched him teetering. "We must maintain order," I said, and swallowed a mouthful of acrid smoke. My throat constricted. "All right"—coughing, I waved him on—"go. Terskan must have some plan up his sleeve. He can fill me in." I squatted and tugged at the door by myself, moving backward, dragging it over the long stretch of the cat, over the grit and rubble. Eikenhorn, the file cabinet slipping by degrees against his hollow chest, stumbled onward, facing me. The door came at an angle between us. "Where will I find him? Who's he with?" The pistol in the leather holster dug into my thigh.

He jerked his head at the station and said something, but whatever it was, I couldn't hear.

I said, with a sharp pull, "Where's Commander Terskan?"

As his thin lips made for a second time the shape of some probably familiar word, an explosion roared out behind him. The whole street flashed white. It was too bright to see. *Time bomb.*

In the next instant I saw I'd let go of the door; Eikenhorn

had dropped the steel file; it was on the ground, on its side, the open drawer fluttering papers everywhere. He was on the ground next to it, trying frantically with both hands to force the folders back in. I turned my attention to the blur of the station house still falling. Hundreds of brown bricks bounced across the cobblestones in the still unnaturally bright light. The sirens didn't change pace.

With a sigh, the walls collapsed. Where they'd stood a cage of red smoke was rising. There was a different kind of shouting from the station now. The cries were so disembodied, they raised chills up my arms. I thought: *Now they are really dying. I don't want to be in charge, not of any of this. I don't want to dig out someone I know. I know them all.* High in the air two huge ravens followed each other, wings flapping through what—moments ago—had been a black, gaping window, but now that there was no molding, no building, they flew unimpeded. They headed into the sun. It was shimmering through the haze of blown dust. Their heads, and then their bulky dark bodies, disappeared in its glow. A moment later only the larger bird swooped down; it was cawing hollowly. So, it was possible to burn up, midair. You thought you were safe somewhere—in the air, in the earth—but you weren't.

I could hardly draw a breath. "Louder, Eikenhorn!" I struck his shoulder. "Answer me! Was Terskan inside the station? Is that where he was when he gave the orders?"

Slowly he lifted a haggard face. "No, the alley." He got again to his feet. "The side, not the back, Commander." Slipping a little, he hoisted the cabinet.

I ran. But the alley, no longer a narrow corridor, in fact not a corridor at all, was a mess. The hosed-down bricks were steaming in the cool air. Soldiers in grey-green uniforms were climbing over the rubble, trying to salvage what they could. They must have been part of the defense, the flak gunners.

"The police commander?" I shouted to the one who'd looked up—a boy with rimless spectacles coated with dust.

"Yes, at your service." He was working to maintain his balance on the debris. The spectacles slipped partway down his reddened nose.

"No, I'm his back-up. I meant have you seen the commander in charge?"

Wearily, brick in hand, he straightened, his blond head breaking into a shaft of sunlight. He saluted me and repeated very distinctly, the glare full in his face, "At your service."

With a groan, I elbowed past him. As soon as I got through the flak group to the other side of the destroyed alley where the squad of firefighters and war prisoners were feverishly pumping air into the station's basement, events become jumbled.

The fire captain: "How many people do you think are down there?"

"I'm not sure of the actual count."

The fire captain: "We can hear shouting—women crying, and we hear men, too, screaming. Are women down there? How many people would seek shelter down there during a raid?"

"There would be women down there, yes."

The fire captain, turning: "Get those animals working!" And to me: "What count do you have of your officers? How many are down there? You can see everything's caved into the basement. Ten? More than that? We're trying to get enough air down to them."

"I don't know. I don't have the numbers. It's the other commander you want, the day one."

The fire captain: "If it's—do we need another pump, Commander, that's what I'm asking."

"Some of them down there were scheduled to be executed."

The fire captain: "But what of your own people? How many of your own people are caught down there now? Give me your best guess."

"Prudmann!" (I saw him.) "That file clerk—we worked together for years, but he's on days now—he'll have a count."

Karl Prudmann was sitting, jacketless, on a dumpster, and his eyes were full of water—so wet those couldn't only be tears. He was singing to himself as the water streamed down his white, doughy cheeks. The front of his shirt looked drenched—no, that much couldn't be tears—but only the result of the fumes. Even when his wife finally died, he'd managed to bear up. Of course, I transferred him to Terskan's shift then, so I didn't see him. I'd known she wouldn't last long, not after her stroke. He seemed to love his wife. I'm not sure now what I felt about mine, about Inge. It's insane, I'd said to her, two years into the marriage. I can't keep listening, I'd rather—look, I can't be with you anymore. I'll send you money, but I need to have some peace. Once I'd gotten over the initial shock of losing the marriage, I didn't actually miss it. Besides, I wasn't about to cry on anyone's shoulder. At night—which can be a time for loneliness—I was busy with my job. When that was done, it was dawn, and I needed to sleep. I awoke in midafternoon and chores had to be squeezed in then—no time for moping. I was lucky I knew how to work things out and spare myself additional grief. Most people don't.

I reached Prudmann. "In the basement," I asked, wheezing like a cheap toy, "how many are down there?"

Silently he looked up, the irises of his eyes swimming.

I turned my head. He'd lost control of himself. "Give me the numbers," I said, looking past him. Painted on the

dumpster in crude black letters was UNAUTHORIZED USE
FORBIDDEN.

"The numbers," said Prudmann, and paused. "Twenty-
four. Thirty-one, with the prisoners."

I hadn't expected that, to maybe lose twenty-four of our
own men. I unbuttoned my collar, chafing from beard stub-
ble, the starch in the cloth, a filthy cold sweat. "Well, all
right, there it is. Go and tell the fire captain what you told
me."

But as he slid clumsily from his perch, I grabbed at his arm.
"Wait a minute, where's Terskan?"

He blinked. "At first—" he mumbled. That's all he got out.
He began to cry. He tried to swallow the sobs, but up they
came. From deep in his throat came the heavy sodden
sounds some old men can make. His shoulders lurched.

"What is it," I said sharply.

"Don't you know? You don't know? It's all, oh—everything's over."

"Impossible." The breath seemed to leave my body.
"You're saying Terskan's dead? You're saying he's gone and
I'm the day commander?"

"You don't know," said Prudmann, and simultaneously a
wild voice burst forth from the end of the alley: "Walter!
Quick! Over here!"

I looked up so fast, I bit my tongue. Crouched in the back
compartment of one of the black police vans was Rolf Terskan. He was hanging on to the roof with one hand and
waving to me with the other. But something was wrong.
Even from twenty meters away, his face looked purpled, as
though he'd just put on a mask with a huge wine-colored
birthmark. "Gruber!" he called. A medic pulled him back
into the compartment. The door slammed. With two me-
chanical burps, the siren on the van started up.

As wretchedly out of shape as I was, I ran. "Halt!" Shouting, I wrenched open the door. "Rolf?" I peered eagerly inside; the van smelled of vomit.

Bloodily clothed, he was lying under a bare bulb with a medic holding him down; another medic had plunged a hypodermic in his forearm. A juicy red bead welled up, sealing the needle to the pasty skin. "Slow—slower," muttered the medic administering the shot. The yellow serum in the hypodermic went down line by line.

I said, "What's wrong with Commander Terskan?" I clutched the door handle.

Terskan groaned: "Nothing." He lifted his head and smiled; his lips were blue-black and his teeth were smashed like cups, like crockery. The bruise *did* seem like a wine birthmark with two dark eyes set in the top of it. He had tiny cuts all over, except for his chin, which was, as always, perfectly shaven. My stomach lurched; Terskan looked just like himself and nothing at all like himself. His smug, handsome, destroyed face.

The assistant who didn't have to keep his attention on the hypodermic glanced over at me. Only his hands and lower arms were clearly lit by the bulb's dim circle of light. Slowly he risked bringing his index finger up close to his ear and made two or three circles; for good measure, he rolled his eyes like a lunatic.

"Nothing," repeated Terskan, dropping his head back with a thud. "Nothing," he shouted, twisting his neck. "She won't even know!"

"What is it?" I demanded. "What's wrong with him?"

"Quiet!" The chief medic withdrew the needle from Terskan's arm. He took a square of white gauze and pressed it directly over the bead of blood. He looked over at me. "He's on his way to the hospital, Commander. Say what you need and get out."

Somehow I crawled in, over his splattered boots. I was

sweating like a pig. "Rolf," I whispered, "they're carrying the files all over town. I don't get it, what's your plan? Why did you give that order?"

"Files," he mumbled.

"Why did you give that order?"

He swallowed; he gave a sigh.

"Don't close your eyes, all right? Don't fall asleep." I wanted to kill him. Oh, he was a real master, wasn't he, pawning the mess off on me? I looked around for help. The assistant had climbed out of the van and left the door partway open. The daylight narrowed to a line that cut across the stained floor and my familiar hand—my fingers pressing against the floor, the brown hairs on my knuckles. "You can't do this now. Wake up. Tell me what you started! What do I have to finish? Why did you give those orders?"

"Call," said Terskan.

"Call?" The siren was shaking the van. "What do you mean?" I waited. "What call? What call did you make?"

Taking a breath, I tilted over his knees. "What call?"

But he didn't answer. Face wide to the ceiling, he lay open-mouthed as a baby; his tongue lolled to one side. "Is it the shot?" I asked the medic, whose back was turned.

He leaned over Terskan, into the cone of light, and shouted at me, "Get out! Now!" He formed a fist and smashed it down onto Terskan's chest. Vomit spurted out of the blue-black lips. I stumbled backward out of the door. The inside of the compartment shutting off, a theater going dark, against my sickening drop back to the alley. The ex-day commander's groans at being called back from the dead— the last thing that made sense. "You tell me!" I shouted. The door slammed shut.

Shielding my eyes, I watched the black van, belching clouds of exhaust, speed away. It passed through the wreckage as fast as it could.

* * *

Roofless and stripped of its windows and walls, the police station still held its captives. Eighteen hours of pumping air into the basement while crews dug through the rubble saved sixteen lives: six belonged to the police, three to the decent citizenry, and all of the seven who, as Aryans convicted of acts of treason and subversion, belonged to the State. The holding cells with their thick uncommunicative walls, had spared the prisoners for their legal executions. That's just the way it is sometimes.

The numbers came out another way, too: twelve police dead in the collapse of the station; another two dead in their own homes—one of them, Leibner, my night clerk—and three, including Rolf Terskan, seriously injured. That left a total working force of seventeen. Not nearly enough to cover the two shifts, not in these conditions. I was going to have to find new recruits or beg other towns for what officers they could spare.

The sun was about to come up, again. Feltz ran over to the automobile in the back seat of which I'd set up temporary headquarters. Behind him the street was lit along one side a sort of fleshy pink. Feltz leaned down, his young face grey, drained of color. I rolled down the window. He said, "Where do you want the prisoners taken, Commander Gruber?"

"Wait." I rolled the window back up and turned to my new clerk. Prudmann had melted away into the night. He'd have to show up for his regular shift, which meant he'd be back soon, at 6:45. It was still dark inside the car. "I need the flashlight, Eikenhorn." I rifled through the sheets on the clipboard that listed the houses still standing nearby. "What about number forty-three? Will it work?"

He scraped through his makeshift records. "Maybe. It has some files, I think." But he took so long flipping the pages back and forth that I snatched them away from him. Most of our contents were listed as being in numbers 43, 49, 55, and 58. The rest of the houses were probably unusable, until we got to the numbers higher up. Those were blocks away.

I rubbed my eyes. Insane. The contents of the station were spread all over town. I had to get a hold of things. I lowered the window. "Number forty-three," I told Feltz, and threw down the clipboard. Even if I couldn't sleep, at least I could splash some water on my face. "All right, I'll tell the residents. Put two guards on those prisoners."

I got out of the car and stepped into a puddle. It was the second day of our unseasonable thaw. The temperature was about ten degrees centigrade. "Come get me if you need me, Eikenhorn." I slammed the door and almost jumped out of my skin. It had been quiet at night, despite the air pumps, despite the work squads, because the blackout regulations still held; any work important enough to proceed could only be done under the moon's slow light; the darkness separated the various worksites, distanced and muffled their sounds. Even those trapped under the surface and frightened of dying called out less frequently for their rescuers. Who knows, probably even *they* had gone to sleep. It was clear that anyone not bombed-out had taken to their beds. Everything had been, essentially, in control—the blessing of night.

At the next corner, debris had been swept up in a pile; balanced like a seesaw atop it was the station's front door. Cursing, I waded into the rubble. I hauled off the door and pieces of glass clinked with the sound of tiny bells. Now the door was scraped. I began to drag it the hundred soggy meters back to the car. "You!" I called to my clerk. "Remember this?" I dropped the weight by the curb. "I ordered you to save this."

Eikenhorn leapt, wild-legged, from the back seat. "I went back for it, after all the files, but—"

"Just save it now," I said. I squeezed a glass splinter from my palm and licked the blood that popped up. My shadow darkened at my feet. Day. The bright time.

Once more, I rang the bell at number 43. Finally: footsteps.

"Who's there?" A woman's voice.

"Police, gnädige Frau, open up."

A fumbling at the lock. In the widening angle appeared a pale round face, red-smudged from pressing for hours against a pillow. "Yes?" said the woman, hiding her body behind the door.

"Morning. I need to come in."

She stood back in the dim foyer, clutching her robe. "Ernst! Ernst, come down."

The foyer was plain: only a bureau, hat rack, an old rug, nothing delicate or fragile in it. Probably any vases or precious knickknacks had been packed away because of the raids. I walked past her, into the parlor. A gloomy space with one of its two windowpanes boarded over with a square of carpet. In the center, roped off, were four of our file cabinets. Behind them, pushed together, were two arm chairs, a brown couch, a small writing desk and chair. Nothing too interesting. But of the three photographs on the wall one showed an elderly couple in Bavarian dress; another, Kreiswald's Citizens' Band posing beneath their banner; the last, a family group of three members—this woman, years younger, a man of medium height, and an infant in a christening gown.

Footsteps behind me. I turned to the foyer and called out, "How is your cellar? Dry?"

The older version of the man from the photo appeared, shoving his arms through his bathrobe sleeves. "Our cellar is dry," he said. He, too, had been sleeping. His sparse hair was mussed up. His neck was pale. It was possible to see his pulse throbbing. The man was too thin-skinned for comfort.

With a sigh, I took off my cap. "Commander Walter Gruber."

In a nasal voice, he said, "Ernst Gelber." Stepping forward, he took the woman's hand. "My wife, Mattilde."

"And your child?" The question came out as if we were friends. But we weren't.

He smiled nervously. "Child? Are you asking about our son, about Georg?"

"Georg, yes."

"Well, he's at the front, we think. We think he's at Stalingrad."

I shook my head. So—right in the thick of it. Half our country's troops seemed to be locked in there; it was all one heard: the enemy's idiotic tenacity, the unending cold.

Gelber said, "But we're not entirely sure he's right at the front. About a month ago, he was; he'd sent us a message through a friend. Now communication's too difficult, although, well, the radio does keep us informed. I'm sure we'll hear soon. We're very proud of him. He's holding down the line for every one of us. It's essential, they say."

"Yes, essential." I cut him off. "Let me ask you something else. Is Georg the one who plays an instrument or is that you, Herr Gelber?"

"Ernst, what is this?" Frau Gelber gave him a worried look.

He paused. "I play," he said, "the trumpet. But it's just a hobby. My real job is with Brunschenfeld—the big leather factory? I'm one of the line managers." He looked at his wife and muttered something under his breath. "We took an oath," he said aloud. "We didn't enter the parlor once you brought in your supplies. We considered the room off-limits for us. Please, inspect anything you'd like."

"No, that's all right. I can see it's in order." With a smile I hoped was reassuring, so I could be done with this, I put my cap back on. "We're taking your cellar now, Herr Gelber, for the time being. We'll want the ground floor, too. You can stay upstairs until you find somewhere else. If you stay, you'll be subject to restrictions."

"But we didn't look, we wouldn't dream of looking. We know our duty," cried Frau Gelber, winding her fingers in the pink neckties of her robe.

"I know. You're good people. We have other matters to take care of now. You have the good fortune of having both an intact structure and a cellar. I don't have the men to spare, not to run all over town for the sake of securing seven prisoners."

Herr Gelber grew pale. "It's a very small cellar." Barely moving his lips, he muttered, "We have to leave, Mattilde, they're putting the jail in here."

"Not here." She looked around at her flocked walls.

"Terrible times, but they say we'll get through them. And so we will. All right?" I paused, dry-mouthed. "Would you mind heating some water? I need to wash up." As I spoke, I opened the front door.

Said Gelber, squinting past me, "Mattilde, it's—they're on their way."

He and his wife edged toward the door. In the new light, a parade was being marched up what was left of the front path. At first glance the line of plaster-coated figures looked as if they were still submerged: the two women with matted, dusty hair and grey faces, the five men with shaven scalps just as grimy; but all were turning their heads about and sniffing at the dawn, their eyes darting here, there, all around, even behind—their expressions buoyant. They'd been locked up so long that the destruction they saw was a gift, a breezy sunlit day. Of course, who could say what they recognized? At one time maybe some of them lived right in these blocks. But all of them looked about eagerly. From the back of the line came a low breathy whistle that rose to a single amazed note. "I want silence," yelled Feltz. "Everyone, forward." Frau Gelber took a long look at the seven prisoners marching toward her and screamed: "No! This is my house, not here! Not in here. No. No!"

"Get control of yourself," I spoke sharply. "This is official business." I put my hand on the leather flap of my holster.

"Mattilde!" Gelber seized her by the shoulders. "Go and heat up Commander Gruber's water." He gave her a little push and turned back with a wavery smile. "She's heating the water."

"Just keep them outside, Feltz!" I shouted, leaning out of the doorway. And in a tight voice to Gelber: "Where's the entrance to your cellar?"

Unaccountably, he hesitated. He didn't take a step in either direction.

"Where do you want them?" called Feltz, as if I hadn't just told him. "Should they be sent around to the back? There are good people on the streets now, going to work."

"Wait a minute!" I snapped. "Keep to orders." I faced again the man frozen in his bathrobe. That silent, shivering man was somehow frightening, the way a squirrel upright in the snow is somehow frightening: its front paws angled stiffly against its chest, its haunches rigid, only the black, popping eyes alive. I said: "They're waiting to be let in, Herr Gelber. Lead the way, yes? Will you do that now?"

He glanced out at the front path and nodded. "Yes. I can do it."

Up from the dark cellar came cartons of mismatched shoes, boxes of watchbands without anything attached, smooth belts looped together by twine inserted through one of their holes. The prisoners, set to work, dumped them in the sunlight in front of the house while Gelber, aghast, went on about how they were rejects from the factory, how he'd been gathering them for donation to the army's Winter Relief effort, for the Russian front—but first he had to find the mate for each shoe, get watches for the watchbands and of course buckles for the belts. His babbling allowed me just to stand there, nodding my head. It was almost as good as sleeping. Back and forth the prisoners stumbled, adding to the hard rubble in the street these piles of soft castoffs. I couldn't stop yawning as I spoke about how these things would be taken later, in his name, for redistribution to the needy. Something good would come of them. And if the passersby thought they could make use of an item or two on their own, all the better; people did stop to see what was going on.

When the basement was emptied, Feltz herded the prisoners into the cellar. He stood at the bulkhead and they went down that way, in single file. As soon as the last head disappeared, he and Müller closed the bulkhead and locked it; they slid the station door across the top, further sealing them in. Now we'd need only one guard posted at the inside stairway to the pantry.

It had gotten to be ten o'clock. Eikenhorn was loping over, heavy-footed, from around the corner. His eyes were shot through with tiny red veins. "They're cordoning off buildings down the street," he said, between gasps. "Herr Oswold just told me the engineers are evacuating the residents of number forty-nine. He came to apologize that he couldn't store our files any longer, since he had to evacuate his flat."

"You mean to say the building is about to be pulled down?"

He paused, flustered. "Yesterday it looked solid—it still does, Commander. We couldn't tell; it takes an expert. The engineer came and said that the internal supports are damaged. Four buildings in the block are roped off. They're cutting off the power now."

"Well, what do we have in there?"

"Herr Oswold told me he has three file cabinets in his flat. Also, five of the evidence crates. Another flat in number forty-nine supposedly has three evidence crates and your and Commander Terskan's desk."

"Supposedly?"

"I have to check."

The winter sun in my face exhausted me. It wasn't human, to keep going like this. People needed to be given some time to gather themselves together and take stock. "All right, retrieve everything," I said. "Who can we spare?"

Eikenhorn looked around, twisting on his long legs, arms limp at his sides. No uniforms in sight.

I said, "Where is your clipboard, Eikenhorn?"

"In the automobile, Commander."

"What are you thinking of?" I snapped. "Keep it with you. You don't have a desk now—you're your own desk." I rubbed my lips, cracked from all the smoke. I thought suddenly of prawns, how to eat them you'd have to lift off the brittle translucent shells from the curled meat. That's what my lips felt like. I hadn't had prawns in at least four years. I hadn't had any breakfast. "Has Prudmann reported in for this shift yet?"

He shook his head.

"He's over five hours late. What about Kremmetz?"

He paused, squinting. "I'm not sure. I might have him listed as working with Sommerfeld; if so, they're probably in the van. Someone reported a trespasser in the Alt Heidelstolz area."

He was no good at it, at being a clerk. Once we gathered together our full records, it'd get worse; he couldn't even keep track of the new ones. I had to find someone who

wouldn't need me to direct every little thing he did, someone who would inform me only of what I needed to know.
No use counting on Prudmann; he shouldn't have disappeared in the first place. Any longer and he'd have to be
listed for pick-up and arrest. "Take Müller with you; he's
guarding the prisoners in the cellar. Bring everything here.
We'll make space."

I went into the house. I headed up the staircase, going
slowly as my eyes readjusted. "Good morning! Wake up!
Morning!"

On the second landing, a door hinge squeaked. "Yes?"
came Frau Gelber's voice, hesitant, subdued.

I was in terrible shape—my heart pounding after only
twelve stairs. I waited to speak until I reached the landing.
"You'll have to find other quarters immediately, gnädige
Frau," I said. "We need all of it." In the gloom, her face
slowly took on its own features. She was more jowly than I'd
noticed in the foyer, her jawline sagging. I continued,
"Leave the front and back doors wide open for us. We'll be
back shortly, with the first of our supplies."

Now I could see past her, into the shuttered room that
held a bed. That it was darkened like this in midday gave me
hope: a quiet retreat, separate from the turmoil outside. I
stepped into the room with a joy there was no longer a
reason to hide. Sleep has a particular smell to it, even in the
day. Ernst Gelber, who'd been lying widthwise across the
mattress, abruptly sat up. He was still wearing his blue robe.
He reached over and turned off the radio, cutting off the
strains of Wagner's *Die Meistersinger.*

"Was that the only telephone," I asked, "the one I tried
before, in the kitchen?" Earlier the phone had been dead.
I'd had to send a messenger to the hospital; he'd returned
with a classified envelope marked for my eyes only: *Rolf
Terskan being kept under continuous sedation; still incoher-*

ent; staff decision: can't risk any free movement—neck, etc. immobilized; many stitches. Will advise of any change.

Gelber looked at his feet; they were hanging down in a strip of daylight. Bony and pale, they were the pathetic thin white of veal. He answered: "It's the only one."

"All right." I wanted nothing more than to lie down. "Well, I know you'll do your part and be quick. It's good for your police if you take away with you as much as you can. Not the furniture, though, not the lamps, or the radio."

This time, as soon as I lifted the receiver, I got a signal.

The SS headquarters in town had a shortwave radio, of course, said their clerk. It was at my disposal.

What nearby towns, I asked him, did yesterday's air raid miss?

Static crackled. Bensheim, he said, and after another burst of static, he said: Passau.

Good, I said. Contact Commander Friedrich at Passau's police station. Tell him I have only seventeen men for both shifts, and no one trained as a clerk. Say I'm relying on him to lend some support. If he can spare even two extra men to help Kreiswald through the recovery period, all the better. But I must be sent someone who knows his way around piles of information. We're drowning in it here.

I told the SS clerk to relay that we'd taken over a civilian house, and gave over the various numbers, so that the station's calls would get rerouted to this phone.

We have a pickup van heading your way, he said—to number 49.

An SS van? I thanked him for his help, but said nothing of our own race to get to number 49. The Gestapo. More of a mess. The moment I hung up, Müller called from the front hallway.

"Where should we put this?" he asked over his shoulder as he backed into the house. He and Eikenhorn had the desk between them. They carried it over to me. "Commander Gruber?"

"Well, look at my beauty," I said, taking heart. The desk had made it through the blast without even one new nick on it. "Something's held up, hasn't it? Set it in the master bedroom. I'll make my private headquarters in there. If you have to, shove it against the bed."

They squeezed onto the staircase. From the second landing came tiny, wrenlike cries of consternation.

I went outside and stood in a square of sun. The lunch whistle blew at the armaments factory on the other side of town. So, this was noon. Most things were going on as before, weren't they? In another twenty minutes, the whistle would open its throat again and the second shift would get out their lunch boxes while the first returned to the work stations. Twenty minutes after that, another group would take its turn. *That's what a system is,* I thought. *Disruptions are absorbed into it. Eventually someone comes to relieve you, then you can eat your lunch. And can go home. And at the right time return to your shift.* It couldn't be long for me now; I wasn't any different than anyone else. I'd be back where I belonged soon enough.

The door swung open and the Gelbers hurried down in front of the officers, the husband and wife each carrying two suitcases. The telephone started to ring. Said Herr Gelber, stepping over a castoff shoe, "Keep moving, Mattilde, keep up."

"You, Müller," I said, and pointed, "you're the new clerk, you answer it. Stay here and field messages."

Spinning on his heels, he disappeared inside. A few seconds later, the ringing stopped.

I slid off the bulkhead. "Let's go, Eikenhorn," I said, taking a breath.

His sparse eyebrows arched, rising into the empty top

third of a pale oblong face. "Commander Gruber?"

"Let's go."

Twenty-four hours after the air raid and the salvage crews were everywhere. What the Allied bombers had started, our engineers would finish, sometimes by wrecking ball, more often by the faster, more precise use of explosives. They had the matter in hand; safety was important. On the street, people went about their business. Of course, there were always those, and not only children, who would stop to watch a detonation. Waiting behind the ropes, their expressions ranged from blank stares to open excitement.

Though I hadn't planned to, once I saw the size of the crowd, I asked for assistance. I selected three of the stronger-looking boys and men and one athletic-looking girl. Eikenhorn lifted the rope. The four volunteers ducked under it.

"Which flat did you take the desk from?" I asked Eikenhorn as I slipped under.

"From the second floor, front, the Wenngarten family." He scurried through. "I can't see any of them now. They had a time of it. The daughter, Thea—of course I asked her name, Commander—was giving the orders to her parents, who wouldn't pack up. They didn't want to leave, they kept complaining that there wasn't a crack anywhere, not in the walls, or the floors. Then all the electricity was cut off and the radio went dead right in the middle of the news bulletin from Berlin."

"Did you hear the news, Eikenhorn? What's happening with the Russian front?"

He grinned; for the first time I'd asked a question he could answer. "The Russians appear to be pulling back. Our defense is working. This could be over soon, any day now. Once they lose, their whole country will be in shambles. It won't be long then."

I shuddered. "True enough, the poor bastards."

"With this behind us, the State might increase our rations." He hurried next to me. "We can bring troops home; our supplies won't all be sent east."

Just then, two SS men in broad-brimmed hats and open greatcoats stepped out of number 49's foyer. "Get back," the taller one said, "there's no time."

Uncertain what to do, the line of civilian volunteers came to a halt. With a salute, I went up to the front. "Commander Walter Gruber. The police have important files in here. These good people are under orders to aid in retrieving them."

The taller of the SS men said, "Commander, our work has priority."

I said, "Yes, well, we need to save the contents of our station, temporarily stored here. Surely the explosives aren't timed; surely someone's controlling them."

Squinting into the sun, the SS man waved his arm over his head. "Bring the van closer," he ordered.

The SS van started nosing its way through the crowd. Hurrying before it, a man with an engineer's insignia on his uniform undid the ropes. In the van came, stopping a half-meter back from the curb. Its exhaust pipe was rattling. The crowd pressed forward again, wading knee-high through the wake of its fumes. In the warm air, you could smell the stink of the exhaust.

"Bring them down," the SS man on the left called into the house. He turned back and said with a pleasantly gap-toothed grin, "Our load first, Commander. It's fantastic what these inspections turn up. After a bombing, there's all kinds of refuse, isn't there? In some ways, the RAF is helping us. It's much easier to round up our Jews after a raid."

"This area was supposed to be clean," I said, surprised.

There was a flurry of feet on the staircase. A woman shouted out, "No! No!"

A dark-haired boy of about twelve, a younger child—a girl—and an elderly couple stumbled out of the dead building into the daylight. They looked completely stunned. Behind them ran a brown-haired, brown-eyed woman, shouting, "No! My children are half-Aryan, their blood is half mine. I have a purity certificate. They're supposed to be privileged."

"Please, Frau Volkmann," said the gap-toothed SS man, "think of your neighbors. They're right in front, watching."

But she said again, "They're half mine. And Frau and Herr Pollack—over sixty-five. Isn't it so, Jews over sixty-five are exempt from resettlement? They've always been quiet neighbors. They're so old, what harm can they do?"

"Step aside, Frau Volkmann," said the SS man.

"You know—did you know he was a hero in the Great War and that's why they haven't been called? And my little girl, see, and my son are supposed to be—please, you must have the wrong house on your list." Somehow she was pushed back into the foyer. "Franzel! Anna! My children!" she screamed. For another moment her cry echoed.

The taller SS man seized the sobbing boy and girl by their wrists. "You can go in, Commander," he said over his shoulder, "but if you want to save anything, you'd better hurry. The whole thing will be gone in just about seven minutes." He pushed the children into the back of the van. "There's a schedule. In, you two," he said to the old couple. "Now."

I said: "Seven minutes?" The crowd, listening, began to buzz.

"Hurry!" Frantically I waved the volunteers into the darkened structure where, on the foyer floor under the bronze square of the mailboxes, Frau Volkmann sat, clasping her own hands. "Take the stairs," I ordered them. "Eikenhorn, show them which flats. Move! Move!"

* * *

The Gelbers' mattress was too soft and rolled me the opposite way I'd expected. In the gloom of the blackout, I sat up and almost pitched forward onto the desktop. The desk was pushed right against the bed. Again, a knock at the door. I clicked off the radio—its low murmurs had seeped their way into my erotic dream. "One moment!" Pulling at my clothes, I went to the window and worked open one of the shades.

Impossible: still daylight. The air had a last hungry glow to it, so twilight would have to come soon. Down the block, a soft explosion. I turned just in time to see a series of mined walls giving way in waves of orderly, almost fluid sheets. From the new piles of rubble the dust rose as languorously as a lady's face powder. I thought again of my reverie: some dark, black-haired woman, her arm across my chest.

Blinking, I buttoned my jacket. "Enter!" My body was dead weight. No use sucking in my gut. A touch of sleep, as anyone knows, is usually worse than full deprivation. It weighs you down more.

The door opened soundlessly. An officer hesitated at the threshold. "Is it Torgood Stella?" I said, trying to focus.

He took a step in and nodded in that curt way. "Commander Gruber."

"Well, of course! Three or four years isn't that long." I came forward. "You made it here in, what, five hours? My god, that's incredible. You didn't come by train, then?" I gripped his hand as if we were brothers.

He was thinner, but everyone was these days. And older—but people were that, too. His hairline had begun to recede, which made him appear somehow thoughtful. He was looking at me with an odd expression in his eyes. Maybe he was thinking what was different about me; I'd had a little mustache back then, but I shaved it off about eight, nine months before—don't know why. I could feel my upper lip curling away from my teeth. I knew I was smiling like a fool.

He said, "We didn't take the train. Some sections of track are out. The roads aren't too bad, so Commander Friedrich sent us here in one of the vans. The driver is signing for a ration of gasoline right now, so he can drive back."

I squeezed his hand again. "How many came with you?"

"Five. They're downstairs registering with Müller. He used to be on the day shift, too. I remember him."

"Of course, of course you do! You're someone who's good at noting even the tiniest detail. How could you forget anything? And Müller's probably filled you in on the challenges in the current situation?" I was overwhelmed to see this man, this unexceptional clerk I'd once cared nothing about. He was part of a time when everything made sense, when responsibility had been sensibly shared. He knew there had to be limits to what could be expected. He knew that a man couldn't be the sole commander, be awake for forty-eight hours, not without others who gave him efficient, unquestioning support. He knew what it took to keep things going. He'd been Terskan's day clerk, the one who knew everything, and had done everything by the book. "Stella," I said, patting the desk, "we're going to make this into Kreiswald's police station. This is our headquarters."

He glanced over at the desk and said nothing. For the first time I noticed there was no chair for it. Clearing my throat, I said, "You're my right hand now. Remember when you wanted to help out on the night shift, when my clerk was having family troubles? That's teamwork. And that cake you had me pass on to him—! Wonderful. There were still little treats in store for us in those days, yes? When was the last time you had something like that, a taste of something sweet?"

He tugged at his jacket; he, too, was sweating in the mild ashy air. He said, "Is Karl Prudmann still alive?"

The question brought me back to the present. After a

moment I answered, "I don't know that he isn't." I turned to the window: clouds were rolling in, but unless the temperature dropped, all they'd bring us was rain. I wanted snow; it was easier to work in snow. I said, "Better put his name down on the pickup list. Technically, he seems to have deserted."

Directly below, the van from Passau was parked in the long last rays of the sun. The driver was pouring gas into its tank; he was using a red can with a black, curved snout. As soon as he emptied that can, he picked up another. There was a third at his feet. He would be able to get back on that.

From behind me, Stella cleared his throat. "Am I dismissed, Commander Gruber?"

I pulled down the blind again. "You just got here, no need to rush. Turn on the lamp. It's next to the radio on the nightstand."

The lamp threw down its little bit of light—before now a small circle which only the Gelbers saw before shutting their eyes. I said: "Well. How is it being back in Kreiswald?"

His eyes slid sidelong to the desk. "I was surprised to be summoned back. Driving in, it seemed that a lot of the familiar markers are gone. There's been a lot of damage." The corners of his mouth twitched. "I think of Passau as home now; it's not a bad place once you get used to it. In fact, I *like* it there, Commander! I haven't thought about Kreiswald for a long time." He looked up again, his face defiant and miserable.

Of course I couldn't blame him. Who hadn't heard those rumors about his wife and Terskan? But Terskan was out of commission. And the wife—Gerda, yes?—hadn't been seen in the town for at least two years. For all I knew, she'd sneaked away from Terskan in order to take up with Stella again! She could be staring out of a window in Passau at this very moment. Anything in the world was possible. Anything.

In any case, her story was of no concern to me. The small detail I was concerned with, after all, was this one man— Stella, standing a meter away from me in a bedroom-turned-office where it was getting on toward night. A good worker, he would hold up as long as I would. Did it matter which other people had once been involved? The past didn't mean anything now. I was caught up in a continuous command and it was all headlong—headlong into the day, into the night. *Headlong!*

"Put Prudmann down on the arrest list," I said, shaking the weariness out of my shoulders. "You're taking over from Müller. Assign him a patrol. When you've got things organized and there's something for me to see, let me see it. For now, set up your post in the parlor. Call me only if there's some emergency." I dipped my fingertips into the tiny pool of lampglow as if it were water from a tap and, making a little show of it before him, cleansed my hands.

For six hours that night, like most everyone in Kreiswald, I slept. It was an exhausted swoon of a sleep. Occasionally, an SS or police siren wailed through the gutted-out silence, but the sound was incorporated into my dreams—dreams that evaporated the moment I awoke to find my legs sprawled over the desk and my arms clinging to a mouth-spotted pillow. It had rained sometime in those few hours; the city pressed against the window was naked and dark. The sky was spread with pink.

I opened the door and went into the hall. As I'd hoped, night had produced a sorting-out of the chaos. Evidence crates had been stacked—though not yet in any order—in the son, Georg's, bedroom. On the first floor, in what had been Herr and Frau Gelber's parlor, Stella had begun organizing our main office area; the hallway to Mattilde's kitchen had been narrowed by a line of file cabinets.

A good, solid, reusable building. You didn't have to be an expert to see its internal supports would make it through almost anything but a direct hit. The only disturbing cracks were in the son's bedroom wall, where two fissures ran up from the floor, behind a map of Europe and Russia, and up to the trim at the ceiling. Because the plaster had a dirty look inside, the deterioration had probably occurred years ago; cracks caused by the recent air raids would probably sift out a purer, paler dust.

So, I was pleased. Number 43 Kempener was a safe place for our station. It also had the benefit of a full kitchen and beds. With a lighter step than I'd had in days, I entered the kitchen. Three of the fresh men from Passau—Vorst, Auersperg and Heimner, they told me—were just pulling on their jackets. It was pleasant to see them, like having a family whose members go out to shoulder their responsibilities without any backtalk. They went out to their patrols. I poured myself my first cup of ersatz coffee.

A pile of folders rested on the breadbox. Idly I glanced at the memo clipped to the top one. Stella's signature, dated February 3, 1943, acknowledged the receipt of six new prisoners. Time of delivery was 3:30 a.m. The State had delivered them when I was asleep.

Stunned, I lowered my mug. How could they do that, send us more inmates, in our situation? Added to the seven who'd survived the bombing, there were now thirteen held in the cellar of this house. They were sprouting like mushrooms down there; in the dark and damp, the men's shaved heads and the women's, well, furred ones would end up by pushing up against the bulkhead. I didn't want to imagine it. I wiped the dribbled coffee off my shirtfront—it was insane.

"Stella," I shouted, stalking toward the front.

He'd been dozing in an armchair in the parlor-office, the boarded-up window behind him. He rose unsteadily to his feet, his eyes—you could see from his expression—still blurred. That black tiny figure in the pupils, that was Walter Gruber. "Commander?" he said, and rubbed his mouth with the back of his hand.

"Pull the files of the seven prisoners, the ones we brought over from the first station house."

"I'll look for them right away."

"Don't just look for them, find them."

One of his curt nods. As soon as he turned away, I despised him. I said, "Where do you think they are? I want the list of their identification numbers, too."

He said, "Yes, Commander." He went into the hall. I heard one drawer after another slide open. Fidgeting, I raised the edge of the blackout blind. The dawn was past; the sun was at the height of the spiked wrought-iron prongs of the fence across the street. A small house had once stood there, but it was reduced to nothing now.

"Commander Gruber," said Stella, coming back in with a quicker step, "I have a list with their identification numbers but no files—not files that match the numbers. Those records might not have been salvaged."

I said firmly, "Of course they were salvaged. The police took the cabinets out of the station."

He said again, "I don't see it, unless the system has changed since I was here. I remember the cabinet reserved for current State prisoners; it was white metal, three-drawer, all the drawers double-locked. I don't see it here."

"The system hasn't changed," I said. "Everything's intact. Look again."

But when he returned, it was the same: he could find none of the current files.

Either the cabinet hadn't been salvaged, so it hadn't been taken to some house—or it had been taken somewhere and somehow forgotten. Which meant our highly classified information was either buried or in the wrong hands. I said quickly. "All right, we'll move on."

A curt nod.

"The dates reserved for execution, do we have those?"

In a low voice he said, "No." He paused. "We have the complete files for the six who arrived earlier in the morning. They were forwarded in the van with them. The driver said to expect more prisoners by this afternoon."

"Stella," I snapped, "that's enough."

He said nothing.

I took a breath. "All right, there's no way around it, since the State hasn't sent a new guillotine yet, we'll have to shoot the traitors, yes? Set up the executions for those seven whose files are missing. Do it immediately, right now."

"Now?" he said. His face stiffened.

I stepped back, away from my own order. "You know what it entails. Just see it through all the way, as you did for Rolf Terskan. We're just changing the method, that's all. We'll do it here, in the cellar."

He looked a little past me. "I'm only the temporary clerk, Commander Gruber."

"I'm temporary—I'm day commander," I said like an explosion.

But his gaze kept going past me, to the boarded-up window. He was supposed to know how to support me. I didn't know anything about this, about handling an execution. Such things didn't take place on my shift. "All right," I said, trying to smile. My hands were shaking; I thrust them behind my back. "Not right now. I'll see what today brings and then make my decision. Besides, it's past dawn."

He looked up.

"Just assign a man to search for the file cabinet. Also we might need other cellars nearby for a series of small prisons, so send someone to ferret those out." I laughed uneasily. "We're going to overflow. But we'll use a rotating guard between them all. We'll end up all right, Stella." Awkwardly, I reached over to pat his shoulder.

His eyes widened. He was surprised, and pulled back a little, but still I'd touched him. It seemed like a pact. "Prepare the forms right away, so we have something to stamp when the time comes," I said roughly.

I opened the front door. Which of the Passau men was that one, the lanky one? "Vorst," I shouted.

He was scuffing through the castoffs. The piles from the Gelbers' basement were greatly reduced, thanks to passersby who could see in the dark. "Commander Gruber?" he inquired, hurrying over.

I ordered him to set up new holding cells. The residents could continue to live on the upper floors of their homes, but they had to help first in emptying out their cellars and boarding up windows. The house structures themselves had to be sound; try to determine that there weren't any possible deep fractures or shifts in the supports. I'd get an engineer to check out the houses he designated.

Vorst nodded. It was his first shift in Kreiswald and he wasn't yet exhausted. He ran to the corner and waited with the pedestrians already there for a line of trucks to lumber past; there were loaded with potatoes from the farmlands. I called at his back, "As soon as you have a cell ready, Vorst, take the six new prisoners out of here and lock them up over there. I want the two groups isolated."

He turned midstreet, and with a curiously flaccid hand gestured that he couldn't hear. The civilians around him were chattering. They were the early birds, out walking with good clean strides. In a house across the way, a blackout blind snapped up. The sun was almost to the level of the second story.

I saw my breath in the air. The air was turning cold again, with the thin edge of frost to it that February always had. The disruption, our three-day thaw, was ending. Things would be set to rights again. It would be winter when it was supposed to be winter. Spring would come when it was to be spring. There would be summer. The system would hold. All the systems would hold.

"Take the prisoners to the first cellar that's ready. I don't care which it is!" I cupped my hands to my mouth. "Hear me?"

Two adolescent girls who were passing in front of me jumped back. One started giggling nervously. I'd shouted right in her face.

"Excuse us, Commander," said the other girl, the blond one. "Come on, Peti." Holding hands, they scurried off, the first girl looking back over her shoulder every few steps. They were going to school, just as they should.

I exhaled. Another cloud of relief. Briefly, I let my eyes close.

Exactly as the lunch whistle blew at the armaments factory, Vorst marched the six state prisoners down a block and a half to the cellar of number 55. I watched from my upstairs window. Then I straightened the covers on the bed and went downstairs.

"Record the name," I said to Stella, "of the family living above our new cell."

"It's already recorded," said Stella, looking up from the white-enameled kitchen table. It was now his desk—and it sat square in the center of the parlor-office. Across it streamed a ribbon of light from the one good window. Stella knew how to handle what was in front of him; he could handle it all.

I smiled. "Well, good. Good work. What else have you done since I was upstairs?"

He said: "Karl Prudmann's been found."

"Where is he? In this mess I could use two clerks who know what they're doing."

He handed me a piece of paper. Outside, a van pulled up, the siren cutting off. There were voices on the street. An order: "Out"—that was probably Kremmetz, there was a northern accent to it—"everyone move!"

I read to myself: *K. M. Prudmann, clerk, Kreiswald Police: Body pulled from river, approximately 5 a.m., 2 Feb. 43. Cause of death: drowning.*

The bulkhead door slammed against the side of the house. He ordered them to march down the few steps. "That idiot," I growled, without looking up. "Tell him: from now on only the paperwork comes here and the bodies go to number fifty-five, right away! When number fifty-five's full, they go over to number fifty-eight. Tell him about our new system, so there's no mistake."

Stella went over and opened the front door. The wind blew in. Hunching his shoulders, arms clasped like an old lady's in front of his chest, he disappeared around the house. "Wait, Kremmetz," he shouted into the wind.

I thought: *The Reichsstrasse footbridge was damaged by the raid. He might have been trying to use it and somehow lost his balance. But I don't know. The current's strong. He could have started anywhere, a different place from where he ended up. No, he couldn't have meant to do this.*

In the glare, Stella reentered, his face red, his nose and lips pinched oddly white. Arms still clasped, he kicked the door shut behind him. I blinked away the last of the light. The corners of my eyes were wet, but it was too late for grief; with my thumb and forefinger I briefly pressed down on the lids. "All right," I said. "I know about Prudmann. What else? Did you get through to the district commander about someone to take over the day shift from me?"

Stella shook his head. "I only reached his aide. He said they're aware of the situation. Until then, he said that he sends his regards for doing a good job."

I sucked in my gut and said, "His regards?" I pulled my head up. Then, startlingly, in an exhalation of almost exhilarating exhaustion, I began to laugh. "Well, well. So they think I'm a Superman! I must be, if my superior says so. Oh, I am! Identify me."

"You"—Stella's face split in a wide grin, the color in his narrow cheeks deepening—"you are Walter Gruber Superman."

"And you?"

He couldn't hold it back. "Torgood Stella Superman, Commander Gruber!"

"Yes?"

He burst out laughing. "Of course!"

And for the first time in the new Kreiswald police station, the day clerk and commander bent over in shared glee. I slapped my holster with the flat of my palm. "Two Supermen, yes?" I laughed until tears rolled down my cheeks. They tasted of something other than salt—the sharp sting of release, of celebration.

Müller burst in. "Commander Gruber—in the street! An emergency, come quickly." The door bounced back against the wall. The wind, empty of everything but cold and daylight, blew in. Then, in the next gust, anyone could hear it: the drum roll, muffled, but sustained. Then silence.

I was outside with the others, standing among what was

left of the castoff shoes and belts. Stella stood at my right. Kremmetz with his bad posture, his gun trained on the—what was it, four new prisoners, five?—had stopped halfway down the block. He turned; the line of prisoners, straggling, chained together, turned. The civilians, clinging to each other's arms in the rising wind, stopped where they were—and they were everywhere, as people tend to be in the daytime: leaving shops, mingling on the sidewalk, in courtyards—they all turned and stopped. It was that muffled drum roll again.

Do you think there will always be some broadcast to warn us, as there was then, that an awful darkness is about to crash down over us?

The newly washed van, still dripping, made its way down the street and louder and louder from the megaphone mounted on its roof came the drum roll and then, low and funereal, the second movement of Beethoven's Fifth Symphony. In a building in Berlin a man was standing in front of a microphone and he was only waiting until the last notes. He took a breath. He said, from the loudspeaker on the van in the middle of the afternoon: "The Battle of Stalingrad has ended. . . . The Sixth Army under the exemplary leadership of Field Marshal von Paulus has been overcome by the superior numbers of the enemy . . . "

What was that, weeping? Everyone in the street, everyone, everyone studied one another. I saw only resolute faces, faces stern and set in stone. From the west, probably back near Ludwigstrasse, came the timed charges of our demolition experts: once, twice. The ground didn't jump where we were—the collapse was far enough away—but against the sky swirled the new clouds of red and pink dust. It looked like a premature sunset, but the sun was nowhere near ready to release its hold. The wind carried the hectic colors even higher.

"We lost the battle," whispered Stella. "With more than 300,000 troops gone, how can we—"

"Get moving, Kremmetz!" I shouted, cutting him off.

Continued the megaphone, " . . . three days of national mourning—then we go on. We see clearly what is against us and still we will not lose. Our brave men . . . "

"Kremmetz!" I shouted, squinting. "What are you doing with those traitors? You have your orders." I unsnapped the cover on my holster. Cocking it, I waved the gun over my head. "Take them to number fifty-five! The family's been told. They know you're coming. Move! Do you hear me?"

"Make way." Kremmetz's voice, thin after the amplified Beethoven and the announcer speaking to us from Berlin, drifted back. In an orderly fashion, the civilians moved aside, and the linked prisoners and then the van were able to ease quickly through them. The loudspeaker clicked off. A temporary disruption, that's all. You could hear the other sounds of the day rushing in: the motors rumbling in the distance, the scraping of the reclamation teams' shovels.

I dropped my arm. To my right, Stella was holding his breath. I caught him staring at one of the women. Just slightly, pivoting from the waist as a marionette would—feet still planted—he turned the upper half of his body in her direction. The shift in his stance was just barely perceptible. I looked again: she was a wincing, light-haired woman with a toddler—a little boy—clinging to her knees. Both were in drab country garb. She stood a good fifty meters away. The fool. I could see it wasn't his wife; she was similar enough, but even accounting for what time does to a person, this was not his cheat of a wife.

"Inside," I said. "We have a cellar to empty."

He looked over at me and said, "Now? Right now?" His eyes were watering.

There are people who won't let things end. That's how it is sometimes. You see it all around you.

I yawned. "All the executions are going to be carried out. Inside. Now, Stella, yes? We're keeping up."

It was a very bright afternoon. By midnight, it had started to snow.

Geheime Staatspolizei
Geheimes Staatspolizeiamt

IV G 2 W. Nr. F.8833.

Berlin SW 11, den   13. April   1942.
Prinz Albrecht-Straße 8

Schutzhaftbefehl

Vor- und Zuname: Johannes Flintrop

Geburtstag und -Ort: 23.5.1904 in Wuppertal-Barmen

Beruf: Kaplan

Familienstand: led.

Staatsangehörigkeit: RD.

Religion: kath.

Rasse (bei Nichtariern anzugeben):

Wohnort und Wohnung: Lettmann, Schlageterstr. 21

wird in Schutzhaft genommen.

Gründe:

Er — sie — gefährdet nach dem Ergebnis der staatspolizeilichen Feststellungen durch ihn — sie — Bestanden des Bestand und die Sicherheit des Volkes und Staates, indem er — sie, ungeachtet einer früheren, wegen seiner staatsabträglichen Haltung erfolgten staatspolizeilichen Beanstandung sein geistliches Amt dazu mißbraucht, durch defaitistische Äußerungen Unruhe und Erregung hervorzurufen, die geeignet sind, den Glauben des deutschen Volkes an den Endsieg und die unverminderte Schlagkraft der Wehrmacht zu erschüttern.

gez. Heydrich.

Beglaubigt:

[signature]

D 42   Schutzhaftbefehl des Kaplans Flintrop, 1942

Secret State Police
Secret State Police Office
IV G 2 W Nr. F 8833

Berlin SW 11, April 13, 1942
Prinz Albrechtstr. 8

PROTECTIVE CUSTODY ORDER

Christian name and surname: Johannes Flintrop
Date and place of birth: May 23, 1904–Wuppertal-Barmen
Occupation: Chaplain
Status: single
Nationality: German
Religion: Roman Catholic
Race (in case of non-Arians):
Domicile: Lettmann, Schlageterstr. 21
is to be taken into protective custody

Reasons:
State Police evidence shows that his/her behavior constitutes a danger to the existence and security of people and state because: Ignoring an earlier police complaint regarding his detrimental attitude towards the State he has abused his clerical position to make defeatist remarks to create unrest and commotion which could serve to shake the German People's faith in the ultimate victory and unfailing strength of our armed forces.

signed:

The Traitor

I WAS A TRAITOR in a time of war. I wanted Germany's leaders to be killed, its troops to be defeated more quickly, the country to come to its senses. Everywhere I looked, people were behaving as if slavery and murder were to be tolerated. There was something called the national good. It entered our lives assiduously, like a whiff of perfume, seducing innocent and intelligent alike; by the end, caught lying with it under our soiled flag, we all stank.

How young was I? Part of me—the Thea Wenngarten who loved books so much she wanted to print them, the Thea who twirled at dances, who dreamed of her future—was young. But the rest of me, caught in the present, was old. The night before Georg was called back to the eastern front I told him I felt that we were but a finite part of an awful, human continuum—we were just part of life's rising and perishing. Hitler with his Thousand-Year Reich promised eternity? Well, let him stay in that hell. It should have held no allure for any of us. Yet almost all the people I knew, almost everyone—

"Thea—"

—they were closing their eyes to the present and promising themselves that, in the end, it would all work out—and the end would be its own reward, so far away, a thousand years away, an eternity away. As if absolution lay there! Vicious fools. What were they doing to themselves, to everyone else? Surely they knew the real cost.

"Thea." My fiancé was whispering my name as a warning. "Thea, stop. It's enough now. Don't keep going with this. Not now, not with me."

But I kept on and, in the night's darkness, Georg's arms wrapped around me. He was holding me in a way that was different from just moments before, as if his embrace were something more than romance—it was a way of protecting me, even from myself. The energy in him. The thin, jumping muscles. I blurted it out then, that I knew he was a soldier, but he didn't have to kill anyone.

"What in the world—?" His short laugh was more sad than dismissive. "I don't have to? Only you would say that." He bit his lower lip. In that habit of his father's I saw for the first time how much he could look like him, like Herr Gelber, a man who tried to outwait his first impulse.

Quietly: "You know you want to say it, too, Georg."

"Do I?" He bent his head and nuzzled my neck. I could feel his breath, smell a moment later the lingering sweetness of wine in it, the cheap half-bottle of Riesling we'd had earlier, now mysteriously transmuted and warmed to something I wanted to gulp down until I found myself sated. He turned slightly. His mouth was near my ear when he said, "I'm out in some field, with guns trained on me, and she's asking me not to defend myself. My Thea."

I shivered as his lips traveled down my neck. This was at the end of August. We were standing out on the back balcony that served mainly as an extra, narrow storage ledge for the kitchen pantry. Behind the closed kitchen door, in fact, sat my parents. In the low wattage of the tiny desk lamp they carried about with them from room to room each night during the hours of blackout, they were reading the *Kompass*. I could almost feel the blunt jabs of their fingers as they went through the pages, pointing out to each other some article that would reassure them, another that seemed, between its lines, to say something quite different, a third that made mush of the first two. They hated Hitler and his gang, and the war, but they didn't know what to do about them. In the circle of portable light, their eyes and hands moved avidly, desperately. I can shut my own eyes now and see them still bending over, my father fifty-three, my mother forty-nine, breathing like one single body—the two heads, the four arms, the round table with its fluttering newsprint wings. The body not grotesque but familiar in its awkward heaviness and its agitation, its inability to stay completely still or fly away.

I pulled back from Georg. Below us, nothing seemed to stir. Our whispers sank into the dark courtyard as if into a well.

Protect yourself from stray fire—hide, bend down, run— but aim at empty space.

You want me to—to ensure defeat?

We both want this war lost.

But I'm exposed. I'm in the field.

In the name of our country! A criminal's country.

I'm against what's happening, you know that. What I've seen, finally, myself. All those people! It's not just words from an enemy's broadcast.

I know.

Wait—I hear something.

Before he finished the sentence, I turned. Across the courtyard the blackout blinds were drawn in the windows of my neighbors' apartments. The whole building was dark.

"The wind," he said, and shrugged toward the elm. The oval leaves, yellow as cats' eyes, turned over together in a second gust.

I looked back at Georg. "You have to." I spoke quietly. "You have to act."

He waited, then lowered his voice; I could feel his words more than hear them. *One is either against the war or not, Thea, we agree.*

Promise me.

I agree with you.

Promise me.

I promise you.

You won't do it, then?

I won't shoot. I promise not to shoot. It's shocking to hear myself say that. Even now.

He shook his head. "Even now," he repeated, then seemed to shake something off—the weight of a long struggle. It would be a new struggle now. We were both in it, already. Georg's face was alight. Touching his cheek, I laughed in relief—that strange relief and amazement. In that moment there was the beauty that we were together.

He whispered in my ear, "I never knew choosing could be this peaceful."

Everything still held, however precariously, to the original pattern. The RAF's raid on Kreiswald, which damaged forty percent of the town, was still five months away. That night, there was still a building across the courtyard. There was still an elm, its branches filled with leaves. Even the door to the pantry was still in one piece, not yet shattered in the detonation set by our own demolition engineers. The air was really very warm that night, when my fiancé quietly tilted his head and smiled at me. Through the pantry door's thin, blue-painted wood we heard: *Children, come inside from that balcony.*

"One minute, Mother. Can we have a few moments more to ourselves?"

Georg pulled me to the iron railing and, leaning against it, we began to kiss. We kissed and then pulled back. The need to see each other was as strong as the need to touch. His intent eyes. The wisps of blond hair near his temples—strays which, baby-sweet, somehow always managed to escape the barber's shears. *Be careful.*

You, too. Don't do anything foolish.

Never foolish.

Thea. I don't want to worry.

You won't need to. Don't.

Those university friends, the sympathetic ones you told me about—

I shouldn't have—

—the ones who secretly debate ideas of resistance, who imagine doing something—how involved with them are you?

I shouldn't even have told you about them. That *was foolish.*

How was it foolish?

Mother cracked open the door. "I've made some tea," she said, beckoning with her ring hand. "Come in with us."

"Now. I want them in here now," said my father, too sternly. Then he called our names in a rich, deep voice; he was enjoying himself, mocking his own authority.

They already had cleared away the *Kompass* and set the table. On the faded green tablecloth with its print of wreathed daisies were four of the good Dresden cups and saucers. The small lamp sat in the center. Its brass head, bowed low at the end of a flexible gooseneck, threw down one coin of light.

Mother said, "I wish I had something sweet to offer you, Georg."

"Next time," said Papa, decisively. "We'll have a real celebration for your return, yes?"

"Very good, Herr Wenngarten!"

Under the table Georg and I were holding hands. I squeezed his fingers.

"Good," confirmed Papa. "I'll keep you to it."

Mother's soft fleshy smile, which had been wavering, steadied. She picked up the teapot. "I'll save the ration coupons. We can have cake," she declared, "seven layers. Chocolate. I would love to bake you a dobos torte, Georg."

"I'd love to devour it," he said, lifting his empty teacup. "I'd love to devour it."

"So?" said Papa, raising his eyebrows at me.

That night in August there was a great deal of teasing and laughter. We were all very happy about our being together. Despite the war, despite what we knew and what we didn't, we were living our lives. And that night we did have fun, don't ever believe that we didn't.

Before curfew, Georg and I started downstairs. At each landing, we stopped and just looked at each other. At the bottom of the stairs, just before the foyer, he said lightly, "You're a soldier's girl, Thea. You know what that means. Kiss me before I leave."

The mingled taste of wine, of black tea.

You'll write to me about everything, won't you?

Every day.

Promise me you won't be reckless, you won't be foolish.

Nor you—you, also. Promise me, Georg.

Oh, god.

What is it? What are you doing?

I can't get you close enough.

A child's giggles echoed from the front entryway. "Look at them! It's Thea."

"Hush," said a woman, lightly.

"But she's kissing him!"

Georg and I, with an embarrassment left over from some other time, a time not embroiled in war, slid apart.

"Don't, Anna," came a boy's cracking voice. "You shouldn't even watch."

"Hush," said the woman, again. "Be good while I check to see if we received any letters."

"The mail came in the morning, Mamma," said the boy—and now I recognized the voice. "Didn't you check then?"

I called, taking Georg's hand, "Good evening."

With a full-throated giggle, six-year-old Anna ducked behind her mother. Franzel stood his ground and said shyly, "Hello, Fräulein." His adolescence, that night, didn't seem so very far away.

"Good evening, Frau Volkmann," I repeated, walking into the foyer.

Frau Volkmann let her mailbox door drop. "Good evening, Thea." Her green eyes flickered over to Georg. She looked uneasily at the medals he had on his uniform. Medals for valor on the field of war.

My face grew hot. I knew what any and all of the uniforms of the Reich must have looked like to her. Five months before, in a roundup of Jewish men, the black-uniformed SS took Herr Volkmann away. My mother, listening through her closed door, reported he'd called out, *Sofi!* She said he was trying to manage the fear in his voice, you could hear it. *Sofi, I'll be all right. I'll be fine, children!*

"This is Georg Gelber," I pressed on. "My fiancé."

Frau Volkmann smiled absently back at me. And touched two long fingers to the base of her throat. The tiny mailbox key, held like a decoration between them, shook slightly.

"Georg Gelber," I continued, "Frau Sofi Volkmann. Georg is leaving for Russia, for the Russian front, tomorrow morning. He's a—a very good soldier, Frau Volkmann, and a wonderful friend. A good friend."

"It's a pleasure to meet you," said Georg. "Thea's told me how much she values having you as neighbors." He waited, then reddened when she didn't respond.

"Mama?" Franzel sidled next to her.

"You see," Frau Volkmann said, quite calmly, looking only at me, "I need to get my sweethearts tucked in." She slipped her arm behind her and brought out embarrassed, round-cheeked Anna, putting her between us. "It's late for them to be up. But the night was so beautiful. You'll have to forgive me, that we can't stay and talk now."

Biting his lower lip, Georg stepped aside. They passed in a rustle of unspoken words. A moment later, the children were running. Their leather soles were pounding and scuffing up the stairs. Midway up, their mother began laughing. "Children, stop. Be good!"

I felt a surge of desperation. "She thinks you're a murderer," I said, helplessly. "An accomplice."

He nodded, white-faced. "I know. I'm afraid she won't trust you as much any longer, Thea. You're this soldier's girl."

I looked at him. But my voice caught. I couldn't go on.

He put on his cap, fixed the visor. We were alone in the front vestibule, before the wall of mailboxes. I took his face in my hands. Or was it that his hands, his warm, beautiful, ten-fingered hands, held my face close to his? That tender vise. Our eyes and smiles were everywhere. Then he was gone.

That was the end of August 1942. I kept my promise to write him every day. I'm not sure whether I kept the prom-

ise to him not to act recklessly. Certainly, I didn't act foolishly. It would have been foolish to act differently than I had.
Foolish not to have stolen: *first*, supplies from the storeroom
of Premier Printers so my university friends could run off
pamphlets against the Nazis—the seditious pamphlets that
later cost five of them their heads by the guillotine; and,
second, files from the cabinets briefly stored in my building
after the RAF bombs destroyed the police station—files I hid
in my clothing and secreted to a girlfriend in Hamburg, who
knew someone else who might make use of them.

In both cases, I was lucky. Not four weeks into my job, my
employer caught me in the storeroom. I was taking two of
the large glass bottles of blue ink from the shelf for my
friends' duplicating machine. My briefcase was open at my
feet. In it rested a brown package of paper, also stolen. When
I heard footsteps behind me, I didn't turn around.

"What? Cleaning, Fräulein Wenngarten?"

I turned in place—blocking the briefcase, I thought. I had
the bottles against my chest, one in each hand. "No, Herr
Breslauer. I was checking our inventory; we're low on some
supplies."

"Are we?"

"Of course," I said, hefting the dark bottles, "everyone's
low."

At that, he bent down. I froze as he pointed at the hem of
my skirt. In the next breath, he wiped his palm across the
fabric, pressing it in between my knees. His hand quick on
my thigh. "Lint," he said, looking up with a thin-lipped grin.
"So, we are low? I'll put in for what I can." He straightened
up, a man proud of his posture. "Give me the numbers when
you've finished, Fräulein," he said, rolling the lint between
his fingers.

The rolling of something tiny between the fingers—yes,
remember that. Everything on the train to Hamburg had a

queasy, nightmare quality: the clatter of the temporary tracks through those stretches that had sustained a bombing, the bulbs overhead wavering dimly on and off, the darkened cities, fields, towns, a black, glittering stream—and in the seat across from me, from Munich onward, a man rolling a child's tooth between his fingers. His still face was shadowed by the kind of broad-brimmed hat the Gestapo affected and by the fur collar of his greatcoat. I tried to forget that I had papers from the police files under my clothing, had them stuffed in, also, among the dirty laundry in the pillowcase I'd wedged beneath my seat. I said, "Good evening" and opened the *Kompass.*

Whenever I looked up from pretending to read, he glanced only slightly away, his fingers working. The unheated train lurching. Soldiers boarding or disembarking in groups. The file papers pressed dangerously against my skin, inside my clothing. The aisle clogged with people sitting on their luggage or directly on the floor. The journey taking until well into the next afternoon because of stopping for ruined tracks. When we slowed down for Hamburg, my companion stood, his hands in his coat pockets. I waited for him to get off, then I left from the second door in the carriage. I waited in the ladies' toilet as long as I could, then headed for my friend's apartment. No one answered. I next went to a small café and took a table there.

Four times, carrying the duffle bag, I crossed the rubble-strewn intersection to go back to her flat. When she finally came to the door and I slipped inside, we had to peel the documents away from my skin. My friend stared at me, then said in a flat voice I should strip completely. Tattoos of prisoner numbers—hundreds of blue ink, reversed-image numbers and letters—had to be scrubbed off me. A soapy cloth did no good; we found a stiff-bristled vegetable brush.

That evening, I returned to Kreiswald. My parents were

already on their way to my aunt's to live on her small farm near Landau. I went off on my own to a series of rented rooms which, of course, no longer exist. There, in one dreary space after another, under the light of the tiny brass lamp I'd salvaged when my parents' building was leveled, I wrote my letters to Georg, sending them off to the East, where I could only hope he was still able to receive them.

I wrote: *Dear Georg, I can hardly bear to think of the hardships you must be undergoing, but I know you—and know you are still honoring your promise to me.*

Dear Georg, I wrote, *The defeats following Stalingrad have been a shock to almost everyone I meet. I promise that we will prevail before long. I'm sure of it.*

Georg, you must know how I miss you, I wrote. *I'm planning for our celebration. Don't forget the dobos torte my mother promised she'd bake us. It will be wonderful.*

I signed letters not with my true name but with a bland endearment, *Your darling.* And I told him one part of the truth, that though I was alone, I was fine. Perhaps he did get some peace from what letters of mine he read.

Of the resisters, there were just a few. It might even be said at this late date that there were perhaps one or two more than a few, but back then it was safe to know only of my small group of true friends and no one else.

After all is said and done, the events I lived through took up a dozen years. Out of all history's shrieks of joy and pain, and out of the silent seamlessness of time, it's these twelve years I must talk about. Was it really that long ago? That long ago when I was lucky to have been a traitor?

Sworn Statement
80-4328

Did you know anyone who was taken away?

Well, did you hear talk of anyone who disappeared?

I mean, back then—did you hear about it, back then?

Some people whispered?

But that is just how people are? You think such filthy things aren't right for anyone to talk about?

And it was everywhere, it wasn't just where you lived? You want me to know that—that it wasn't just where you lived.

Tell me, what were people saying when they whispered?

You didn't listen?

So, you read the *Kompass* back then, and back then it said nothing?

Then, what did you—what did you learn from the newspaper, other than about the decapitated bodies in the basement?

The prisoners' bodies—the ones in prison uniforms, yes. Other than about them, what else did you learn that surprised you?

No, afterward, after the war was over. What other things did you learn from the newspaper?

Tell me about what happened outside Kreiswald, that one time.

It was near the war's end, and—?

You say people were found—buried? You mean Jews?

So, Kreiswald didn't have many Jews? You think not even two hundred. At the most, one hundred fifty, one hundred sixty?

But the majority of those who were buried outside of town, were they Jews?

They were? But they must have been from elsewhere—strangers? They weren't the Jews that anyone knew?

Could there have been others buried with these Jews that one time, do you think?

Maybe a few Germans who were criminals? Anyone else—?

Anyone who—maybe some homosexuals? Maybe a few gypsies and such? Some religious and politicals?

What else did the newspaper say about this event, besides that these strangers, these people were buried outside of Kreiswald?

What else do you remember?

I understand you don't like to talk about such things. Can you tell me why you don't?

Filthy?

And did—no, take a moment, it's all right. Take a moment.

Take a moment.

You—you want to live a good life? Things were hard for you? There were things happening all the time? And you—you had people to care for? Things were happening every day, even in your own life—you have only one little life! You have people to care for—

Take a moment, then we'll go on.

Better?

Better now?

If you want—all right. All right, what happened outside Kreiswald that one time? What did the newspaper say happened?

The Americans were advancing?

There was nothing left at the end, and—the war was almost over? And when there wasn't gasoline for burning, they had to push the people down in the pits. You mean, buried alive?

Is that how they were killed?

Others knew—wait, the others recorded—the others buried them?

Why did they—the others—do this, tell me.

They didn't want the Americans to see? Who didn't want that?

You don't recall any names, but—good people. Good citizens. They were—I must understand they were people with professions—people who played in the band? Yes, and who were educated? Shopowners and housewives—and the police and such?

You read this in the *Kompass*? How did the *Kompass* learn of it?

It was reported by the Americans?

How did the Americans know, if the people were already buried? Did they learn from the files they seized? Didn't you say they'd gotten hold of some files?

But why wasn't the event in these files, when so much else was recorded—the other information you told me about?

This was at the end—yes? And the files—the statements in the files—they were from when there was time for recording such things? Prisoners' confessions? All that?

But how did the Americans know what happened to the Jews and others outside of Kreiswald? If it wasn't recorded—if the people were buried alive before the Allies arrived?

So, they weren't covered completely? The dirt was still loose around them?

You say: there wasn't enough time for such a task. The dirt was everywhere? They weren't completely covered? It was all just terrible. It was medieval—you say it was nothing a person—it was a grotesque—

Take a moment. I'll wait.

No, take a moment.

All right? Good. Now tell me what happened, then.

So, the victors—the Americans—made everyone— those townspeople who were nearby—the Americans trained guns on them?

Then—?

The citizens had to go back to that place outside of Kreiswald and—? Yes? And you had to dig up the bodies—

Not you. Right, the citizens who were nearby. The citizens who were still left.

So, they dug everything back up? Then they had to rebury the bodies? But not—not on top of each other, you say? This time, one by one?

I see: they were laid out again, one by one.

You say: this is very good, it is decent.

You say: such things often happen during wars.

Just a few more questions. Is that all right? A few more?

Wait. All right?

Well, when you learned about the exhumations, how soon afterward was it?

Since it wasn't very long afterward, what did you do? For instance, did you go there once you found out? Did you visit the graves?

You didn't? It wasn't the place for you?

Did you want to find out who made that decision to murder the people right outside your town?

What didn't you want to know?

Well, are any of the people responsible still around?

Where are they?

Are they nearby?

Wait. I have one or two more questions. I—I'm still in the dark. You know what that means, to be in the dark? It's a saying, yes.

Let me just ask one or two more.

How did you react when you discovered the people in charge are still living around you, right here?

All right, I'll rephrase it. Tell me: how typical is your town?

I know you live here. You need to be comfortable. You—you live as best—

I'll rephrase it. If you would—

You don't want to? I'll rephrase it—tell me—

You weren't part of anything bigger? Kreiswald is home?

Let me rephrase it. Why did you—

All right. Here's a release.

No, you just sign it. No one can tamper with it, it's your statement. I'll sign it, too. I'll swear to its truth. Then it goes in our files.